Turning, h
fireplace, Git
of the room. 'It's wonderful.

'Yes.'

'And will it all be yours one day?'

'Mmm.'

'Then I think you ought to marry me. I would *love* to be chatelaine of all this.'

'Would you? The roof leaks.'

'Oh.'

'The drains need replacing, the walls repointing, it's freezing in winter, freezing in summer…'

'And you don't want a wife,' she stated mournfully.

'No.'

A little smile in her eyes, she walked across to him and slid her arms round his neck. 'Then I best settle for mistress, hadn't I?'

'Yes.'

Emma Richmond was born during the war in north Kent when, she says, 'Farms were the norm and motorways non-existent. My childhood was one of warmth and adventure. Amiable and disorganised, I'm married with three daughters, all of whom have fled the nest—probably out of exasperation! The dog stayed, reluctantly. I'm an avid reader, a compulsive writer and a besotted new granny. I love life and my world of dreams, and all I need to make things complete is a housekeeper—like, yesterday!'

PRAISE FOR EMMA RICHMOND:

of THE BACHELOR CHASE:

'Emma Richmond entertains with wit and strong emotional intensity.'
Romantic Times

of MORE THAN A DREAM:

'A unique romance…Richmond has a magic way of making you wait breathlessly for the next hurdle and its tragic outcome or glorious victory.'
Affaire de Coeur

'Emotionally charged, thought-provoking… A true love story.'
Romantic Times

HIS TEMPORARY MISTRESS

BY
EMMA RICHMOND

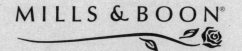

First published in Great Britain 1997
Harlequin Mills & Boon Limited,
Eton House, 18-24 Paradise Road, Richmond, Surrey TW9 1SR

© Emma Richmond 1997

ISBN 0 263 80611 1

Set in Times Roman 11 on 12 pt.
01-9802-40183 C1

Printed and bound in Great Britain
by Mackays of Chatham PLC, Chatham

PROLOGUE

BROAD shoulders propped up against the wall, a rather cynical twist to his mouth, Henry Sheldrake watched the young woman waiting to go before the cameras. A modern-day Helen who could launch a thousand ships before breakfast if she felt so inclined. She probably didn't, he thought with a dry smile; ships would be rather small fry to the girl who had launched a giant cosmetic company's expensive advertising campaign. Although, at the moment, she looked as though she'd be unable to find her own feet without help, which surprised him.

He had rather expected that the astonishingly beautiful Milgitha James would be constantly poised. Certainly that was the impression Cindy had given him. Tough, ruthless, and determined to make her mark on the world. And yet Cindy liked her. Said they'd been friends since school. Why? It had always been his experience that most females didn't like beautiful women, so what was it about Milgitha James that inspired liking in Cindy? Inspired lust in himself?

Smile twisting wryly, he continued to watch her. Thickly lashed hazel eyes, and dark brown curly hair with an impossible shine. He hadn't been able to stop thinking about her since the first time he'd seen her face on the screen.

As though aware of being watched, she turned her head. Her eyes widened, clashed with his, and he almost felt the little gasp she gave before she turned quickly away. Clever Milgitha, he applauded silently. The startled glance, the flushed cheek, were far more appealing than outright flirtation. If they were genuine, of course. Which, in this case, they probably weren't.

Nothing Cindy had said had led him to believe that the delectable Miss James was shy. And yet he wanted her. Wanted to touch, and feel, and taste. Fastidious and selective, he'd met other, far more beautiful women, and they'd left him cold. Milgitha didn't. She invited—fantasies. He'd been watching her for weeks—a fact she knew very well—and now, he thought, it was time to actually meet her. Put the fantasy to rest.

Or not, as the case may be. He wasn't particularly busy at the moment, and a chance meeting here in the studio shouldn't be put to waste. He couldn't remember the last time he'd pursued a woman—they usually pursued him. God knew why. Being eligible and wealthy didn't make him a better person. But then, most women of his acquaintance didn't care about the nice, only the wealthy.

You're a cynic, Henry. Yes. And bored. So very, very, bored.

CHAPTER ONE

FLUSTERED, Githa whispered urgently, 'Who *is* that? Everywhere I go lately, there he seems to be.'

'Henry Sheldrake,' the assistant grimaced. 'And I'd stay away from him if I were you. The man's dangerous.'

'Why?'

'Because he is,' she insisted.

'But who is he?'

'A literary agent, here to hold the hand of Peter Marshall.'

'Peter Marshall?'

'The author. He's being interviewed now.'

'Oh,' Githa murmured absently as she continued to watch him from the corner of her eye. Long and lean, aloof, elegant. Brown silky hair and an air of infinite boredom. A man she'd seen several times over the past few weeks. A man who was beginning to worry her.

Already nervous, because live television always made her nervous, she now felt excited, which was absurd.

'OK, let's go. Ready?'

Jerking back to the assistant, she stared at her in bewilderment.

'Time to go,' she repeated. 'And *don't* get involved with him. That man is trouble. He doesn't *like* people.' Escorting Githa into the studio, she gave her a friendly pat on the arm, a comforting grin, and pushed her in the direction of the stairs that led onto the set.

She didn't remember the interview, barely remembered what she'd been asked, what she had answered; her mind remained fixed on a tall man with silver eyes. A man that made the heart shiver. And when she walked off the set, a vague smile still on her exquisite face, he was waiting for her.

Heart pounding, eyes wide, she just stared at him.

'You said you intended to write a book,' he stated coolly.

'What?'

'Just now.'

'Did I?'

'Yes.' And the way he looked at her sent every sensible thought out of her head.

'I'm a literary agent.'

'Yes.'

He handed her a small white card. 'Come and see me. We'll talk about it. Where do you live?'

And, like a fool, she told him.

He nodded, and walked away. Cool, dismissive, arrogant. But the expression in his eyes had been... what?

She didn't know how long she stood there. It felt like ages, and then a sound intruded—laughter—and she blinked, looked down at the small piece of cardboard in her hand. Henry Sheldrake. Who was dangerous.

'Still here, Githa?'

Swinging round, she stared blankly at the assistant. 'What?'

'I merely asked if you were still here. Rhetorical,' she grinned, 'because obviously you are. What's wrong?'

'Nothing,' Githa denied automatically. 'Why is he trouble?'

'Who?'

'Him. Henry Sheldrake.'

With wry exasperation, the assistant stared at the beautiful girl before her. Taking her arm, she led her over to the mirror and made her look at herself. '*That's* why he's trouble! Look at you! From nine to ninety, he puts the same look on the face of every woman he meets. And it *bores* him!'

'Does it?' Githa asked almost wistfully.

'Yes! Don't yearn after him; I don't think he likes women. Certainly, from what I've heard, he doesn't treat them very well. He tramples sensibilities, hopes and aspirations into dust. Brutally. Go home, Githa. Forget him.'

Forget him? Sensible advice—and she wondered why she felt unable to follow it. The other times she'd seen him, he hadn't actually looked at her. She'd looked at him, though, and his mere presence had made her shake.

Glancing at the assistant, she saw the wry smile in her eyes. 'You too?' she asked softly.

'Oh, yes. Me too,' she agreed. 'The first time I met him...' With an embarrassed shrug, she continued, 'He looked at me, and I couldn't look away. Hope springs eternal, doesn't it?' she murmured with soft self-mockery, 'And for one long moment I was trapped in a land where everything seems possible. That the charismatic Henry Sheldrake would tumble helplessly into love with me. And then he turned away, walked off as though I didn't even exist. I couldn't stop thinking about him for *weeks*.'

Smile turning wryer, she murmured, 'Pathetic, isn't it? And whatever it is he's got it shouldn't be allowed.' Silent for a moment, as though she still thought about him, she finally gave herself a little shake. 'I have to go; take care of yourself.'

With a vague nod, Githa walked on and out to the car park. Tall, elegant, beautiful—and a fraud. Because the person inside wasn't *anything* like the outer packaging. But people made assumptions based on that packaging, and, because of her job, her high profile, she had to *pretend* she was the way everyone thought her, because that was what she was being paid for.

And the car park was dark, she discovered. Nearly empty. With a quick look round, she began hurrying towards where her car was parked in the far corner. The darkest corner. And heard footsteps.

Heart beating over-fast, eyes wide, frightened, she

ran. She'd been hearing a lot of footsteps lately. On
dark pavements, by the house, at night. Hands shaking, she managed to open the car door on the first try,
scrambled inside and locked the doors. And she hated
it, this fear. This inability to confront whoever was
stalking her.

Firing the engine, she drove quickly away, eyes on
the rear-view mirror. But she saw no other car following her and so gradually relaxed, and thought instead
about the enigmatic man with grey eyes.

She drove to the hotel she'd been allocated, asked
the doorman to park her car in the underground car
park, and booked in. The staff were flatteringly atten-
tive, and she felt depressed. Yearned to be herself.
Grin. Do something totally outrageous. But she was
being stalked, and victims tended to—hide.

She ate in her room, went to bed early, felt momentarily safe. And, despite the fear, it felt as though
she spent the whole night thinking about Henry
Sheldrake, literary agent. She felt excited, thrilled, a
little bit frightened of the way he made her feel. That
man was dangerous. She didn't ever remember wanting a man before. But she wanted this one. Crazy. Or
perhaps not. Perhaps it was because she was so desperately in need of a white knight. A champion. And
he was certainly the stuff of which champions were
made.

Early the next morning, she drove home.

Tired, longing only for a shower and change of
clothes, a long sleep—because she hadn't slept at all

well the night before—the sight of a police car, two policemen and her neighbour standing outside her house almost made her drive on, seek the sanctuary of another hotel for the night. Almost.

Drawing to a halt, she stared at them. They turned to stare solemnly back. Now what?

One policeman walked forward. 'Miss James?'

'Yes,' she agreed warily.

Consulting his notebook, he intoned, 'Miss M. James?'

'Yes. Githa.'

'Geetha?' he queried dubiously.

'Yes. Short for Milgitha. What's happened now?'

His sympathetic smile looked more like a grimace. 'Best come and see.'

Eyes worried, feeling slightly sick, she climbed from the car—and saw what had happened now. CHEATING BITCH had been sprayed across the front of her house in large bright scarlet letters. And, whether intentional or not, the effect was made worse by the fact that the red paint had run in places, was dripping down the walls like blood.

No one said anything for a while; they all just stood and stared at it.

'Likes paint, doesn't he?' Githa murmured inadequately. 'The last time it was yellow, thrown over my car. The time before that blue, poured through my letter box. When did it happen?'

'We don't know exactly. A patrol car came past at just after midnight and it wasn't there then. Your neighbour rang us a short time ago. We can't keep a round-the-clock watch,' he apologised. 'Don't have the manpower.'

'I know.' With a deep sigh, she turned to the young constable beside her. 'Thanks, anyway.'

He nodded, looked as helpless as she felt. 'There's nothing to go on, you see.'

'I know. Malicious phone calls were easier,' she said lamely, and with a small attempt at a joke. Not that she felt like laughing. She hadn't felt like doing that for a long time. 'It's escalating, isn't it? First the phone calls, then disgusting letters pushed through my letter box. And if I hadn't had the phone company intercept my calls, the mail company intercept my mail, perhaps he wouldn't have taken up art work.'

'And I didn't hear *anything*!' Jenny, her neighbour, exclaimed. 'I'm so sorry, Githa.'

'Not your fault. Be nice to know what it was I *did* though, wouldn't it? Who it was I supposedly cheated. You don't need to wait,' she told the policeman. 'There's nothing you can do, is there?'

'Sadly no. Until we know who it is…'

'Yes.'

He made a vague movement towards his cap, not quite a salute—not quite anything, really—and turned to rejoin his colleague in the car. 'If anything else happens…'

'I'll let you know,' she completed softly.

'Someone else came,' Jenny murmured, with the air of one who wished to get all bad news over in one go and was terrified that she would be the messenger who was shot.

'What?'

'A few minutes ago. I don't know where he went… I mean, his car's still there.'

Turning to look at the gleaming silver Mercedes parked a little way along the road, and not recognising it, Githa shrugged. 'Someone being nosy I expect.'

'Well, he didn't look *nosy* exactly,' Jenny began, and Githa was astonished to find her friend actually blushing. 'He was, um, well, really rather dishy. You know, one of those men who make you feel—desperate.'

'Desperate?'

With a weak smile, she added, 'Boneless. Oh, Githa, he was the most amazing-looking man you've ever seen. A bit bored-looking…'

Sudden alarm inside, she whispered cautiously, 'Bored?'

'Yes,' a cool voice said from behind them.

They both swung round too fast, Jenny with mortification, and Githa with astonished shock; she felt her heart miss a beat.

Pale grey eyes with a dark ring round the irises regarded her without expression.

Flustered, she turned away, stared once more at the front of her house. Felt stupid. Unprepared. Shaken.

'Not very nice,' he commented softly. 'There's nothing round the back.'

Feeling decidedly uncoordinated, she creakily turned her head once more. 'What?'

'No graffiti on the back of the house.' He nodded to Jenny, moved Githa to one side—a touch that sent her whole body into shock—opened the gate, and walked up Githa's path to the front door. Extending one elegant finger, he touched it to the red paint.

'You *know* him?' Jenny gasped. 'I've never felt so mortified in my *life*! I mean, he must have *heard*!'

'Yes,' Githa agreed faintly as she stared rather worriedly at the man on her doorstep.

'So who *is* he?' she persisted.

'Henry Sheldrake.' Dangerous Henry Sheldrake. 'I'll see you later. Thanks, Jenny.'

'What for?' she demanded comically. 'Allowing a stalker to paint your house?'

With a faint, absent smile, Githa walked towards the waiting Henry. Felt—displaced.

'Githa!' Jenny called urgently, and she turned, retraced her steps.

'You do *know* him?' she asked worriedly, voice pitched low so that Henry wouldn't hear.

'Well, yes...'

'Only—well,' she added determinedly, 'if I hear any noises from your house—any noises at *all*—I'm coming round!'

'But he can't be the stalker!'

'Why not? Because he's good-looking?'

'No, of course not. But he's a literary agent. Well-known, respected. And he'd hardly boldly walk up to

me if he was stalking me, would he? Thanks, anyway.
I'll see you later.'

He couldn't be the stalker; it was absurd. Avoiding
eye contact with the patient Henry, she opened the
front door, ignored—or tried to ignore—the fact that
he followed her, and walked along the tiny hall to the
kitchen. Her heart was beating far too fast, and she
felt dizzy. But an effort had to be made, didn't it? She
was Miss Varlane. Cover girl of the year. Competent.
Sophisticated.

Right. As sophisticated as a dung beetle, she
thought near-hysterically. But what did he *want*? Fantasising about him was one thing. Having him here in
her house was quite another.

Sitting at the table, she arranged her expression into
one of competence, focused her attention on her
hands. 'Double glazing, wine salesmen, religious
freaks, *catalogues*...'

'Is it a conversation?' he enquired smoothly as he
leafed through the accumulated junk mail he'd picked
up from the basket outside. 'Or a soliloquy?'

Irritated, bewildered, she turned her head, stared at
him, watched him sort through the circulars and free
papers. 'What?'

He didn't even glance up as he strolled towards her.
'Conversation requires response, soliloquy doesn't,'
he murmured drily. Placing the pile beside her, he
walked across to the phone and lifted the receiver.

'Oh, please, just make yourself at *home*,' she derided sarcastically.

'Thank you.'

'And you don't actually have to *tell* me what it is you're doing!'

'Ringing a decorator friend of mine to ask him to come and remove the paint from your front wall.'

'You don't need to! I'm perfectly capable of doing so myself!'

'Of course you are,' he agreed mildly as he continued to tap out numbers.

Mouth tight, she glared at him. There was nothing worse than being agreed with! Especially when the other person sounded so insufferably smug! And the assistant at the studio had said he didn't like people, didn't like women. So what was he doing *here*? 'I don't even know what you're *doing* here!' she complained.

'Passing,' he explained unhelpfully as he presumably waited for the phone to be answered at the other end. 'My office isn't far from here. I saw what had happened, and stopped. As anyone would.'

No, anyone wouldn't, she denied crossly to herself. Anyone with any sense would have driven on. 'Have you just driven down from Manchester?'

'No, I came down last night.'

'I wish I had,' she murmured morosely. 'Then it might not have happened. Or I might have seen who did it.'

'Yes.'

Mouth even tighter, she stared at his profile. Aristocratic, she decided. And an air of civility that would

chip granite. Cool, remote, faintly uninterested. Fin-
icky. Not a charmer; he certainly didn't set out to
make you feel at ease. He just—was. A watcher. A
waiter. And disturbing. Yes, very disturbing. 'And do
you know how very *irritating* it is to have a multitude
of inflexions injected into one short agreement?' she
asked pithily.

He ignored her, began to speak softly and economically into the phone. And, even if he had been just
passing, he hadn't had to come *in*, had he? Poke his
elegant nose into things not his concern. He'd said to
get in touch with *him*!

Worriedly waiting until he'd finished, she stated
with a great deal more aggression than was required,
'You said to get in touch with *you*.'

Replacing the receiver, he leaned back against the
wall. Watched her. 'Mmm.'

'And the girl at the studio said that you—' Embarrassed, she broke off.

'That I…?' he queried helpfully.

'It doesn't matter,' she muttered.

'Was the most hated man in London?'

'No! No.' Absently banging her heels together, fingers beating out a jittery tattoo on the table-top, she
murmured, 'She merely said that you were—a literary
agent,' she concluded lamely.

'And that I was admired, envied, scathing of fools,
and not much liked by my contemporaries? That I had
a cutting tongue and an indifference to criticism?'

'No,' she mumbled. Merely that he was dangerous.

'How long has this been going on? You mentioned double glazing, religious freaks.'

Abandoning her heel tapping, she looked down, picked at a loose splinter of wood on the table. 'Three months. He, whoever he is, started off with heavy breathing down the phone, then threatening mail— deliveries I didn't want, *salesmen* I hadn't asked for— nuisance value more than anything else—and then this started. Footsteps in the night, paint on my car, paint through my letter box…which is why I had it sealed and a basket put by the front door. Jenny usually empties it when I'm away.'

'And the police can't do anything?'

'No. They patrol as often as they can, and they staked out the house for a while, but they don't have enough manpower to do it permanently.'

'And you have no idea who he is?'

'If I knew who he *was*,' she exploded crossly, 'I'd…' What? she wondered. Kill him? With a deep, *aggravated* sigh, she flung herself back in her chair, glared at him, then had to look away from light eyes that were far too penetrating for her peace of mind. 'I won't let him *beat* me,' she muttered. 'Three months! How could someone even be *bothered*?' she queried in bewilderment. 'It isn't as if it does them any *good*! He can't *see* what it does to me!' And it was affecting her work, her social life…

'Calm down.'

'I am calm!'

'No, you're not,' he denied drily. 'Pieces of you keep twitching.'

With an irritated shrug, she demanded, 'Well, what do you expect? It's *frightening* me! The moment I get home… Madrid, all last month, I drove to the studio straight from the airport, and I'm *tired*!'

'Go away for a while.'

'I am!' she muttered grumpily. 'A friend of mine has lent me her cottage for a while.'

'Where?'

Glaring at him, she said forcefully, 'Oh, I'm really likely to tell you that, aren't I? *You* could be the stalker for all I know!'

'Not my style,' he denied softly. 'Who's the friend? Cindy?'

Astonished, she just stared at him, and he smiled, a trace of humorous mockery in his grey eyes. 'How do I know Cindy? We're old friends.'

'Since when?'

'Oh, since for ever. She's never mentioned me?'

'No.' And don't *do* that! she wanted to yell at him. Don't talk to me in that soft, affected drawl when I don't know what you *mean*, what you *want*!

He looked at her with *something* in his eyes, but *what*? *Was* he attracted to her? As she was attracted to him? It was so hard to *tell*. No man had *ever* made her feel this confused before.

And he'd done the same to the girl in the studio— and then just walked away. She'd also said that he didn't like women. That he confused *all* of them! Was he secretly laughing at her? Waiting for her to make a fool of herself? He was dismissive, ironic, slender and elegant—and he made her feel stupid. And breathless; he made her feel as though she was the only woman on this earth worth talking to.

Confused, muddled, she tried to remember where the conversation had got to. 'Did Cindy tell you to get in touch with me?'

'No,' he denied in the same soft, disturbing voice.

'Then why did you? And don't give me that garbage about giving me your card because I stupidly said I might write a book when whatever-her-name-was asked me what I'd do when my current assignment was over!'

A small gleam of amusement in his eyes, he murmured admiringly, 'And all without a breath.'

'Look!' she exploded. 'I'm not very good with innuendo, with ambiguity! If you're trying to tell me something, please just say it!'

Watching her, waiting, a faint smile in his eyes, he murmured, 'I want you.'

Shocked, she just stared at him—and the cool appraisal from silver eyes stopped the breath in her throat, made her look hastily away. 'Don't be absurd.'

'Why is it absurd?'

'Because it *is*! You don't know me!'

'But want to,' he said softly. 'Ever since the first time I saw you—you fuelled a fantasy that wouldn't go away. I wasn't intending to do anything about it,' he said rather self-mockingly, 'because fantasies are usually best left as fantasies. But then Cindy told me that she knew you, that you'd been at school together, and the fantasy seemed…'

'No!' She was shaken, out of her depth, because men didn't behave like this. Not bluntly! They didn't come up and say they wanted you! They took it slowly—a smile here, a letter, *something*… And did Cindy know about this? 'Does Cindy know?'

'About how I feel? No.'

'She didn't ask you to look me up?' Grasping at straws, she shoved her hands through her hair, gripped her scalp hard—wanted to run away before it was too late.

'No. Go to the cottage,' he urged quietly.

Staring at him, then as quickly away, eyes still puzzled, frightened, she murmured, 'You said you'd known her for a long time.'

'Cindy? Yes.'

'But…'

'But?'

'Well, I don't know, do I?' she demanded, irritable all over again.

'Neither do I.'

'What?'

He smiled. Small, economical, but a smile. 'She lived near to us when she was a child. Her home life wasn't very happy, and so she would come along to our house. Popped in and out like a jack-in-the-box.'

'I knew she was adopted, but—'

'But we didn't know she had a friend called Githa

James until you fronted the advertisement for the air-line.'

'Didn't you?' she asked foolishly. Wanted her?

'No. I was at home, which I very rarely am. Lucinda had come up for the weekend. The commercial was on the television, and, because I knew that she worked for the same airline, I asked her if she knew you. She casually informed me that you were at school together.'

'But she had never mentioned me until then?'

'No.'

But then, there was no reason why she should have. And none of this had anything to do with him wanting her. With a confused sigh, she stated quietly, 'We were best friends. Still are.'

'Yes. And now you're Miss Varlane, cover girl for the giant cosmetic company.'

'Yes, and I wish you'd go away,' she said worriedly.

He smiled.

'*And* you've been following me! You might not be the man who's stalking me, but you've definitely been following me, haven't you? I've seen you several times over the past few weeks.'

'My office is just round the corner,' he said blandly.

'Then it's very odd I haven't seen you *before*!'

'Is it?'

'Yes!'

'Go to the cottage,' he repeated quietly.

'I *am* going!' Slapping her hands flat on the table,

she pushed herself to her feet, went to stare worriedly from the window. Was aware of him behind her. Aware of every blessed breath he took!

'Don't worry about it,' he soothed gently.

'How can I not worry about it? I don't want you to want me! I don't need any more complications in my life!' And yet...

No! He excited her.

'Go to the cottage. Think about it. We can talk when you get back.'

'Yes,' she agreed hastily. Anything. She would agree to anything that would get him out of the house. Looking up, her eyes collided with his, and they skidded away as though frightened. 'I don't understand any of this,' she complained.

'Don't you?' he asked softly. Almost suggestively.

'No,' she denied. But she did. That was the trouble. She wasn't totally innocent, but no man had ever made her feel like this. So sexually aware. He didn't frighten her—she frightened herself. Because she wanted him. And if it had been possible to measure the electricity in the room the needle would have been way off the scale.

He looked like every fantasy hero any woman had ever had. Was his air of boredom cultivated? she wondered. To intrigue? If so, it was working very well. Tall, slender, classically good-looking—and that floppy brown hair you positively yearned to push your fingers through. And if only he wouldn't look at her she would probably be able to cope. Almost cope. But

if he ever touched…placed that well shaped, uncom-
municative mouth against her own…

'Fantasising, Githa?' he asked softly.

'What?' Eyes wide, she frantically shook her head.
'No!' She was behaving like a no-brain. Where was
the sophisticated, cool Miss Varlane? Summoning up
every ounce of composure, she gave him a haughty
look—what she fervently hoped was a haughty look.
'I think you'd better go. As you say, we can talk when
I get back.'

He gave a dry, mocking smile.

'I'm off balance at the moment,' she continued
firmly. 'You know, the vendetta and everything…'

'Mmm.'

'And I'm not normally like this.'

'No,' he agreed.

'Shut up!' She was normally cheerful and uncom-
plicated, but the last three months had put an enormous strain on that cheerfulness—and that was *all*
this was. Normally she would have coped with Henry
Sheldrake like a—well, like a veteran! But because of
this maniac she'd become edgy and impatient—irritable with Jenny, hadn't *seen* Cindy for weeks—and
all because of a vendetta she didn't in the least understand.

She didn't recall that she'd ever done anything to
anyone to make her the target of so much malice. And
she didn't know how much longer she could go on
pretending that everything was all right. That she
could cope. 'So you see…'

'I see very well.'

'Well, I hope you see the same as I'm seeing! We'll talk when I get back.'

'If I still want to.'

Mouth tight, still keeping her distance from him, she gave a regal nod.

'Then, if there's nothing more I can do…?'

'No,' she replied. 'Thank you.'

'The decorator will be here in about an hour.'

'Decorator?'

He smiled. Economically. 'To remove the art work.'

'Oh.'

He gave a lazy wave and sauntered out, closing the front door quietly behind him.

Collapsing at the table as though all her bones had been removed, Githa clenched her hands tight together to stop them shaking. Oh, boy. And he'd been laughing at her. Well, he would, wouldn't he? she thought despairingly. He'd probably expected someone sophisticated, worldly, and instead had discovered a worm. Well, he wouldn't be back. Why would he come back? She hadn't even been articulate! She would never have coped with him anyway. A man like that was way out of her league.

But why had Cindy never mentioned him? She'd thought they told each other *everything*! They'd known each other since they were eleven. Two little girls cast adrift at a large and imposing boarding school.

Two little girls who had become best friends. Left school together, joined an international airline together, become hostesses. And now Cindy worked on the flight desk at the airport—or had done the last time they'd spoken—and she was face of the year, Miss Varlane, cover girl for the giant cosmetic company. And all because she was—photogenic. Because the camera loved her. Because of luck, and being in the right place at the right time.

And now some maniac wanted to punish her for that same luck. Destroy her peace of mind. Only he wasn't going to be allowed to, she vowed. It had been a chance in a lifetime. Unimaginably lucrative, it had allowed her to buy this house, do things she had never dreamt of doing—and she was not going to let him spoil it.

She determinedly ignored the little voice that told her that she didn't even *like* being Miss Varlane.

And, now, here was Henry, who wanted her. As you want him. No, I don't. Yes, you do. With a small squeal of irritation, she banged her hands on the table. Stop it, Githa! Just stop it!

With a deep, troubled sigh, she stared at the junk mail he'd placed tidily beside her, wished she were more—experienced. Idly sorting through it, she found nothing threatening. No nasty letter reviling her. Sometimes weeks went by without anything happening. Sometimes something happened every day, sometimes more than once a day, but, today, nothing else.

And, hopefully, in Cindy's cottage in Shropshire, there would be a little peace.

Getting to her feet, she depressed the button on her answer machine, listened to the messages, and quickly returned the calls. There was no message from Cindy. She tried ringing her, but her phone remained unanswered. She'd try again in the morning.

Face still slightly troubled, she went out to collect her suitcase from the car, avoided looking at the art work, then carried her case up to her small bedroom. She loved this little mews house—the fruit of her labour—and he wasn't going to spoil it for her, whoever he was.

Dumping her suitcase on the bed, she walked into the bathroom, shedding clothes as she went, and, when she'd showered, removed every trace of make-up. She sat at the dressing table, and stared at herself in the mirror. Then smiled, stuck out her tongue.

She didn't think she was beautiful, she was just— Githa. Quite nice eyes, she thought dispassionately. Nice smile, or so she'd been told. And lovely, clear skin, but nothing exceptional. Nothing at all like the girl who looked out at the world from advertising hoardings, television commercials. Without the make-up, the fashionable clothes, no one ever recognised her. People sometimes said she *looked* a bit like Miss Varlane, and she always laughed, made a disclaimer, because she didn't *want* people to know.

She didn't know why, or how, it happened—just that on camera, film, she looked different—more alluring, sexy, luminous. Not that she *wanted* to look like her alter ego—she didn't. She had enough trouble as it was. And she didn't *like* being the centre of attention; she sometimes found it an unbearable strain. It was not what she'd set out to be.

And now there was Henry. Another complication in a life that was littered with them. But perhaps he wasn't a complication. Perhaps now that he'd met her face to face his fantasy would be over. She found the thought depressing.

A faint flush on her cheeks, she quickly withdrew a band from the dressing-table drawer. But there would be time to think about Henry. Time in which to come to terms with the way he made her feel.

Scooping back her hair, she moisturised her face, and then went to put on clean underwear, loose, comfortable trousers and top, before she set about unpacking and sorting out the dirty washing—a constant chore when she was always travelling.

The decorator duly came—but she didn't let him in. She made him a cup of tea, thanked him for coming so quickly.

'Get a lot of these,' he informed her laconically. 'Wouldn't believe some of the stuff people spray on walls. Want me to mend this security light?'

She shook her head. 'It shines in Mrs Gordon's window opposite and so I keep it switched off. Not that they're much use. People get used to them, don't

they? Like burglar alarms. After a while, no one takes
any notice.'

She paid him, thanked him again.

The next morning, as she was carrying her case out
to the car, she saw Cindy, and smiled when she saw
her friend hurrying along the mews.

'Hi,' she gasped breathlessly. Holding the stitch in
her side, she leaned on Githa's railing for a few sec-
onds to get her breath back. 'Overslept,' she grinned.
Eyeing the suitcase, she asked hopefully, 'You *are*
going?'

'Yes.'

'Good. And you have the directions? Number for
the burglar alarm?'

'Yes.' She smiled. 'And why are you chasing along
the road? Where's your car?'

'In for a service.'

Still smiling, she shook her head at her. 'Need a
lift?'

'Would you? I'm going to be hopelessly late for
work as it is.' She helped Githa put her case in the
boot, and climbed into the passenger seat, opened her
bag, and began to put her make-up on. 'The sign of
a true friend,' she grinned. 'That I should come out
in public without make-up just to see a chum off on
holiday.'

'Thank you,' Githa said solemnly as she negotiated
the heavy morning traffic in London.

'How was Madrid?' Cindy asked. 'How was the
television interview?'

'Madrid was tiring, the interview nerve-racking.'
Githa smiled.

'Serves you right. How do I look?'

'Terrific, as always, although how you can put mas-
cara on in a moving car I'll never know.'

And, by the time they reached the airport, not only
did Cindy have her make-up done to perfection, but
her uniform hat firmly in place and her scarf artfully
arranged, and no one would ever have known she had
dressed all by guesswork.

'I'll see you when you get back. Have a good time.'

'I will, and thanks again. It means a lot to me.'

'You're welcome. That's what friends are for.'
With a last wave, she walked into the airport building,
and Githa drove on towards Shropshire.

After following Cindy's precise directions and instructions, she bought groceries at the village shop,
then drove up the long, rutted track to the cottage,
meticulously shutting all gates behind her. At least,
she *hoped* it was the right cottage; Cindy hadn't actually described its appearance. And the building she
could see peeping out through the trees ahead of her
didn't look very much like a *cottage*. It looked—big.

She'd already made a fool of herself in the shop by
grizzling, all because there had been a little girl outside, crying. No noise, no sobs, just silent tears trick-
ling down her grubby face—and her own eyes had
filled with sympathetic tears. She couldn't help it.
Crying children *always* made her cry. Even *reading*

about a crying child made her cry. She'd make a
hopeless mother. And now, if this was the wrong cottage, she was going to make another fool of herself.

So, what else is new, Githa? She *wasn't* sophisticated, or sexy. She wasn't even very experienced, but
people assumed she was. Assumed a glamorous life-
style denoted an equally glamorous—or at least experienced—private life. But she was *ordinary*. Inside,
she was very ordinary indeed. And she still found it
bewildering, this life she was forced to live. This—
lie. Would she eventually become this person everyone thought she was? That was the worrying thing.
That the transition might happen without her even no-
ticing!

With a deep sigh, she stared at the sheep. Cindy
had mentioned sheep, hadn't she?

Sheep gave way to ploughed fields of red earth, and
then she was in the tree line, and the left fork that
would take her to the cottage. Parking on the ce-
mented base, she climbed out, stretched, stared at the
cottage. It was rather Tudor-looking.

Behind her was a steep, tree-covered hill, in front
of her stretched the valley. She could see what looked
like an old manor house tucked into a fold of the
hill—empty, perhaps, derelict—and, apart from the
intermittent bleating of sheep, it was blissfully silent.
No cars, no radios, no—nothing.

Approaching the front door with some trepidation,
she only relaxed when she had punched in the alarm
numbers and nothing untoward happened—no shrill

blast of a burglar alarm. It was big, she discovered. Large lounge with an enormous inglenook fireplace, dining room, fully equipped kitchen with dishwasher. Downstairs cloakroom. Three large bedrooms upstairs, and a bathroom. And here, she thought happily, for two weeks she could be who she liked. No make-up, no smart clothes—no stalker. Just peace. Peace she sorely needed.

For the next few days she explored the immediate countryside on an old bicycle she'd found in the shed, drove into the delightful little town of Ludlow, met the farmer, investigated the local pub. And on Saturday afternoon, following the instructions found in the cottage, she replenished the woodpile. Dressed in a woollen shirt, jeans and comfortable trainers, she was happily, and very inexpertly, sawing logs—until she became aware of being watched.

CHAPTER TWO

SHE swung round too fast, lost her footing—and Henry, with a speed that astonished her, tossed the jar of coffee and newspaper he'd been holding into a nearby bush and caught her.

Leaning her safely against the side of the wood-shed, he stared down at her. He wasn't even breathing hard.

She was.

'You frightened me,' she whispered, and never, ever had she been more conscious of the nearness of a male body, of the warmth of hands that still held her shoulders.

'Sorry,' he murmured, his eyes never once leaving hers.

Swallowing hard, she blurted raggedly, 'What are you doing here? You said we'd talk when I got back!'

'Did I?'

'Yes! You're not sharing the *cottage*?' she stated in horror.

'Aren't I?'

'No!' she wailed. Had she *totally* misunderstood?

He smiled. Just a faint, amused movement of his mouth. 'No,' he agreed, 'I'm staying at the Hall.'

'Hall?' she whispered.

He pointed towards the old manor house. 'Don't tell me you haven't investigated?' he mocked.

'Well, yes—I mean, I know there's a house there—but I didn't go too close. I didn't know who lived there.'

'I do.'

'You do?'

'Mmm. And I don't lend milk or sugar,' he warned softly.

Didn't lend... 'Henry!'

He smiled, then gently, and very deliberately, pushed a tendril of damp hair away from her forehead.

She shivered.

'I didn't hear a car.'

'I didn't use the car. I arrived late last night. I've just walked up from the village.'

'*Walked?* It's four miles!'

'Eight,' he corrected. 'Four miles each way.'

He must be fit, she thought inconsequentially as she continued to stare, rather mesmerised, into his eyes. And he *hadn't* said he was coming here.

Still frowning, worried, heart beating much too fast, unable to move away, unable to do anything, she continued to watch him. Old jeans, old workshirt, no coat. And he *still* looked elegant. Fastidious. Made her conscious of how sweaty she was, how untidy.

'What were you doing?' he asked mildly.

'Doing?'

'Mmm.'

'Oh, sawing wood. Cindy's list said to keep the woodpile stocked.'

'Yes,' he agreed slowly.

'But you didn't expect that I would?'

'Could,' he corrected after an infinitesimal pause.

Aware of her restricted breathing—as he must be—she took a funny little breath, tried for flippancy, and failed. 'I can do lots of things.'

'Yes,' he drawled very softly, 'I imagine you can. Drop the saw.'

Fingers suddenly nerveless, she dropped it.

'And the log.'

She only vaguely heard the soft thud it made as it reached the ground because her ears seemed filled with the sound of pounding blood.

'I'm all sweaty,' she said thickly.

He didn't answer, just moved his eyes to her mouth—and she felt extraordinarily ill.

'I've seen Cindy,' she babbled.

'Here?'

'What? No. The morning I left. I gave her a lift to the airport.'

'Kind of you,' he murmured absently as he continued to stare at her mouth.

'Yes.'

He gave a faint smile, moved his hand, began to rub his thumb slowly and hypnotically across her bottom lip.

'Henry…'

'Be quiet.'

Staring fixedly at his throat, heart beating like a trip-hammer, she grunted when he deliberately rested

his body against hers, felt, rather than heard, the wood
creak behind her as too much pressure was applied.

And then he kissed her. Lowered his mouth, and
slowly kissed her. Savoured the taste of her.

Hands clenching agitatedly on his shirt-front, she
gave a little jerk, a little gasp.

Lifting his head, he stared at her, and his eyes, for
once, looked almost sleepy.

'Surprised?' he asked softly.

Looking away, she gave a jerky nod, a frantic shake
of her head.

'Expecting to be bored by it?'

'Bored?' she asked dazedly. 'No.' Barely aware of
what she was saying, she asked weakly, 'Were you?'

'No,' he denied languidly. 'But then I always knew
that I wouldn't be.'

Glancing at him, and as quickly away, she whispered, 'Did you?'

'Yes.'

'But you haven't known me for always.'

'Oh, I think I have,' he drawled. He untucked her
shirt, placed warm palms either side of her ribcage,
and she dragged in a sharp, shuddering breath. Forgot
to breathe out.

'You're shivering.'

'Yes,' she gasped. 'You make me nervous.'

'I know. Kiss me.'

An almost painful wrench in her stomach, eyes
wider, worried, as she stared anywhere but at him,
she pleaded indistinctly, 'Henry...'

'You knew this was coming. From the first moment

we met, you knew. So don't play games. Don't play hard to get. Kiss me.'

'I didn't…wasn't… Oh, God.'

Hands still clenched on his shirt-front, deciding that the effort required to unlock them was too great, she shuddered, moved her eyes to his mouth—and a little groan escaped her. 'Oh, Henry, do you have *any* idea what this is doing to me?'

'Yes.'

I'm not like this, she thought in bewilderment. Not this inarticulate. Not this *shy*. But she did want to kiss him. Wanted to lose herself in this man. Wanted to feel all the things she had never felt. Wanted that beautiful mouth against hers.

Unconsciously parting her lips in anticipation, she leaned slowly towards him, touched her mouth to his. Closed her eyes.

Feeling so very unlike herself, she moved slowly against him. Unclenching her fingers, she slid them up to his neck, his nape, threaded them through his silky hair, explored the shape of his head. Her breasts touched against his chest and the nipples, already hard, began to ache. Pressing closer as excitement laced through her, she felt the strength of his thighs against her own, wanted more.

He moved to accommodate her, pressed one thigh between her own. Pressed hard.

Boneless, hypnotised, aroused, wrapped in the warmth of him, the strength, unaware of the cool wind that blew off the hill behind them, the bleating of sheep, the call of the birds, she continued to explore

his mouth, allowed him to explore hers. Pressed
against him. Felt urgency begin to stir as she revelled
in the warm, spiralling ache inside. Shivered.

His hands slid to her back, held her against him,
urged her closer when she shifted at the feel of his
growing arousal.

'Take it off,' he urged thickly against her mouth.

Feeling faint, unreal, she whispered in perplexity,
'What?'

'Your shirt. Take it off.'

'I'm not wearing a—'

'I know.' When she didn't immediately comply,
merely shuddered, he moved his hands, began to undo
the buttons himself. He didn't fumble. He might be
aroused, his breathing slightly erratic, but he didn't
fumble. Ignoring her weak protests, her half-hearted
attempts to stop him, he slipped the last button free.

She held the shirt together. He tried to ease it apart.

Staring into his eyes, half-defiant, half-frightened,
she asked shakily, 'Suave, sophisticated Henry, making love in a field?'

'Why not? We all have our fantasies.' He sounded
bored.

'*More* fantasies?'

'Yes.' Eyes holding hers, he unclenched her fingers, and spread the shirt wide.

Heart skittering erratically, cool air on her exposed
breasts, she dragged in a shuddering breath as he
looked down. And then someone called him.

'Henry?'

His whole body stilled. Tilting his head back, he

closed his eyes, drew in a deep breath through his elegant nose, and slowly released it.

'*Henry!*'

Tucking her shirt over her exposed breasts, he turned and walked away.

Left shaking, head resting back against the hut, she forced herself to take deep, slow breaths, and then began to hastily do up her shirt. Aching with tension and frustration and need, she couldn't believe she had allowed him to do that. Could so easily visualise how it might have been if someone hadn't called him away—*would* have been. And it excited her. There would have been no objection, no refusal; she *knew* that. Because she *wanted* him.

With a long shudder, not thinking, not even knowing *how* she felt, she walked away. Climbed up towards the trees and just kept going. When she came across a fallen tree, she sat as though boneless, rested her head in her hands. She felt exhausted, clammy, slightly sick.

She knew when he arrived. Not by sound, or any other giveaway sign; she just knew he was there. 'Who was that?' she asked, curiosity getting the better of her. When he didn't answer, she turned her head and found him standing not three feet away, leaning against a tree.

'You frighten me,' she whispered. 'You meet people, like them, get to know them, and it's a slow, nice, gradual thing. It's not like this. Not—desperate. I don't know how to cope with you, Henry.'

He gave a wry, twisted smile. 'I'm not sure I know how to cope with myself.'

'Sorry?'

Levering himself away from the tree, he walked towards her, seated himself beside her. 'You've become something of an obsession, Miss James. Ever since Lucinda told me who you were, I've been—haunted by you. I would stare at your face on the hoardings, watch you on the television, and mock myself for a fool. And then I saw you in a book shop...'

'You weren't looking...?'

'I was looking.'

'But you said...'

'Yes. And then I saw you in the studio, and I knew the feelings weren't going to go away. I wanted you.'

'But I don't look *anything* like I do on the television,' she pointed out in bewilderment.

'No, you look exciting, and aggressive...'

'I'm *not* aggressive,' she protested.

He raised an eyebrow, and she blushed.

'Not normally! I've been under a lot of stress lately.'

'Mmm.'

'And I'm not like the woman on the hoardings...'

'It's you,' he said softly, 'not "a woman".'

'But it isn't! I'm not *like* her!'

'Aren't you? Then why do your eyes send messages that your body denies?'

'They don't!' she gasped.

'Yes, they do. I look at you, and I want you. That simple. That complex. And even when I don't look at

you I want you. As you want me. Don't you?' he
asked softly.

'I don't know. I don't feel very well.'

'Because of me?'

'No. I think I ate something. I feel…' Sick, was
how she felt. And ill. Lowering her head, she swallowed hard, rested her forehead on her knees.

'Not the effect I usually have on women,' he
drawled, and she gave a weak smile.

'No,' she agreed. 'I don't suppose it is.' She knew
it wasn't. The girl in the studio, Jenny…

He felt her forehead, frowned. 'Come on, let's get
you home.' Helping her to her feet, he put one arm
round her for support. 'Can you walk?'

She had no idea. Probably. And he didn't sound
very concerned, did he? Just really rather detached.

'We're going the wrong way,' she protested a few
minutes later.

'The right way,' he corrected.

Even more nervous, she dragged to a halt, stared at
him. 'I don't want to go to your home.'

'But that's where I want you.'

'But I can't have an affair,' she protested weakly.
'Can't afford one until I finish my contract with
Varlane. There are clauses…'

'Who will know?'

'*I* will.'

Staring down into her worried face, he moved one
hand, traced her nose, her mouth. 'I imagine there are
clauses about adverse publicity, about being discreet,
but nowhere will it forbid you to have an affair. I

know about contracts, Githa—and I can be very discreet. Come.'

And such was his power, the hypnotic effect he had on her, she made no more protests, but allowed herself to be led towards the Hall. But it didn't stop her thinking, worrying about it.

She glanced fleetingly at his profile, tried to find some—softening there, and was unable to. He looked almost stern. Forbidding. Not in the least lover-like. Moving her eyes away, she stared ahead, watched as the Hall came into view. From a distance it looked like a ruin. Old, rambling. Close to it looked—mellow.

Still feeling ill, shaken, she whispered, 'How old is it?'

'Begun in 1241,' he drawled casually. 'I don't think it ever got finished, although I believe the original family gained a licence to crenellate in 1291.'

'Oh, crenellate,' she agreed weakly, and he smiled.

'Mmm. But as you can see they never did, or, if they did, it all fell down. It was rebuilt after the Civil War, and we've been adding and subtracting ever since.'

Well, they would, wouldn't they? People like that. A whole different world, wasn't it? Was he wealthy? She had no idea. Not that it mattered. 'How long have your family lived here?'

'Since seventeen hundred and something.'

She suspected he knew *exactly* the date. Was that all part of the glorious game? Never boast? Be casual about it all? 'My family lived in their house for seven years,' she murmured. 'That didn't have crenellations either. But then, I don't suppose they had a licence.'

He halted, stared down at her, gave a crooked grin. She gave a wry little smile back.

'But I don't suppose that your family's house had the guttering falling off, the brickwork crumbling, and plumbing that would make a civilised man weep?'

'No,' she agreed.

'Still feel sick?'

'A bit. Perhaps it's a panic attack.'

A gleam of amusement lit his eyes as he led her through the last of the trees and helped her down the rutted track towards the rear of his home.

They passed a tumbledown stable block.

'Houses the tractor,' he said laconically.

A broken greenhouse.

'Awaiting restoration,' he murmured.

She tripped on a broken cobble, glanced at him sideways, and he gazed at her with the bland expression of a fool.

A dog howled. Mournfully.

'Hound of the Baskervilles,' she murmured, then gave a funny little shrug.

The howling turned to excited barking, and she wondered if life really was preordained. Perhaps on the day she'd been born all this had been written down. That on such-and-such a day she would meet a man named Henry Sheldrake. That she would allow him to take her to his home. Seduce her.

'Don't look so worried.'

'But I *am* worried!' she exclaimed.

He merely smiled and opened the back door, which wasn't locked. 'Nothing to steal,' he informed her, straight-faced. He guided her through an arrangement of wellington boots, garden equipment, replaced a jacket that fell off as they brushed past, and opened another door that led into the kitchen. 'The dogs won't hurt you.'

She halted, glanced at him. 'Dogs? Plural?'

'Mmm. Two. The family are away for a few days.'

'"Family" being…?'

'My mother and her husband—my stepfather.'

'And so you're here to feed them?'

'Mmm.' And seduce my new neighbour, his eyes seemed to say.

Flushing, she preceded him into the kitchen. And the dogs became miraculously quiet.

She stopped, stared at the two sitting canines—a black Alsation-cross, who sat like a regimental sergeant major—alert, at attention—and a border collie, who just looked anxious.

'They look guilty,' she murmured.

'Probably been on the furniture.' He clicked his fingers. The Alsation lay down, and the collie squirmed forward for a pat. Githa giggled.

He glanced at her, lids heavy, eyes appraising, and she flushed again. 'You can have tea without milk and sugar,' he drawled. 'Or coffee without milk and sugar.'

'Your coffee is still in the bush,' she pointed out.

'So it is.'

'And you don't lend milk and sugar because you don't have them?'

'No. I have to feed the hounds, give them a run. Are you hungry?'

She shook her head.

'Thirsty?'

'I'll have water.'

He nodded, collected a bottle from the fridge and handed it to her. 'Make yourself at home. Have a shower if you want to. First room at the top of the stairs. Lounge is through that door.'

Feeling awkward, confused, *nervous*, she walked into a lounge of ancient splendour. Everything for comfort, not style. Everything old. The television standing in the corner looked incongruous. The fire was low—a guard protecting the hearth—and she walked across, added a log, gave it a prod with the poker. There were photographs on the mantelpiece, on the piano—on every available surface, it seemed. A large room—cluttered, homely.

Sinking down onto the sofa, she stared at the fire, sipped at her water. Why did he want her to have a shower? Because he was intending to carry on where he'd left off when someone had called him? Go home, Githa. When he takes the dogs out, go home. Back to the cottage.

But she wanted him. Wanted him with an urgency she had never felt before. Wanted him inside her, and felt heat suffuse her body at just the thought of it. But it wasn't love, nor even liking. Just—desire. Attraction. She didn't know him, nor he her. She wasn't a virgin, not totally inexperienced, but she had never felt like this. Wasn't *ready* for this. But she did want him.

With a deep, worried sigh, she screwed the cap back on the bottle of water, made sure the guard was properly in front of the fire, and left the house. Hurried along the track to the cottage.

What would he think when he found her gone? Nothing. Probably nothing. But she felt nervous in the cottage, unsteady as she made herself a cup of tea, then went upstairs to shower. Shrugging into a warm towelling robe, she padded into the bedroom—and found Henry there.

Startled, wary, heart beating too fast, she stared at him.

He stared back.

'You ran away.'

'I...'

'Come here,' he ordered softly.

She shook her head.

Face still, without expression, he moved towards her. 'How do you feel?'

'Much b-better, thank you,' she stuttered nervously.

'So formal?'

'Henry...'

'Shh. You talk too much.' Reaching her, he gently pulled her against him, stared down into her anxious face. 'I want you,' he said simply. Untying her robe, he slid his arms inside, held her warm body against him, watched the little flare of excitement in her eyes, the doubt, the fear.

'You arouse me,' he stated softly. 'Just the thought of you arouses me. I watched you hurry away, like a thief, and I wanted you. Wanted you naked. And I wanted to gaze into those amazingly beautiful eyes where every thought, every feeling, is mirrored. Undress me.'

Hot, breathless, she protested weakly, 'Henry...'

'Your body's warm, soft, pliable, and I want to feel it against my nakedness, not against my clothes.'

'Henry, we don't *know* each other!'

'No,' he agreed as he continued to stare down into her beautiful eyes. 'I'm not promiscuous, not a womaniser. In fact,' he added with cool deliberation, 'I have been celibate for quite a long time because most women don't interest me. But every once in a while along will come someone who does. A woman who excites me. The way you excite me. And I want to make love to you. Now. And you want it too. Don't you?'

'I don't know,' she admitted weakly, but her body was melting against him, wanting. 'You make me feel as I've never felt before. Your voice is soft, hypnotic, and I find myself behaving as I've never behaved before. And you make me feel inadequate. Stupid.'

'Do I?'

'Yes.'

'And do you know how you make me feel?'

She shook her head.

'Out of control. Undress me, Githa,' he urged, and his voice was huskier, warmer. Persuasive. 'One but-

ton at a time, one belt, one zip. I showered—quickly,'
he added with a disturbing smile. 'You're on the pill?'

She gave a jerky nod.

'And you want it as much as I do, don't you?
Don't you?'

'Yes,' she whispered.

Breathing uneven, feeling faint and really rather
loosely woven, she moved her eyes to the top button
of his shirt, and her hands moved to obey his instructions. One button at a time.

'It's nice to know you aren't as unaffected as you
appear,' she murmured unsteadily. 'Your heart's skittering all over the place.'

'Yes,' he agreed as his mouth touched against her
forehead, her hair. 'You smell of woodsmoke.'

'It's the fire.'

'I know.'

And his muscles were tense. As were hers.

Undoing the last button, she pulled his shirt loose
from his trousers, stared at his chest, took a shuddery
breath, and allowed her breasts to brush against him.
Staring up into his face, she searched his eyes, moved
her hands to his belt buckle, felt the indrawn breath
he gave as her knuckles brushed his stomach.

'Deliberately slow, Githa?' he asked thickly, 'Or
just frightened?'

'Not frightened,' she denied, 'just… Oh, dear God,
Henry,' she breathed, 'this is all happening too fast!
And I don't *know* you.'

'Pretend you do,' he murmured. 'Pretend we've

been lovers for a very long time. You want me to use protection?'

Did she? she wondered dazedly. She had no idea.

'Do I need to?' he persisted softly. 'How many lovers have you had, Githa?'

'One,' she said shakily. 'Two years ago. He's married now,' she added with helpful foolishness. 'With a little girl.' Her breasts were aching, and there was the most awful clenching pain in her stomach, a moistness inside. Raising her eyes to his, feeling so very out of her depth, she didn't know what else to say.

'Zip,' he prompted.

Without taking her eyes from his, she fumbled for his zip, quickly slid it down, and gravity took care of the rest. He heeled off his shoes, stepped free of his trousers and pulled her back against him.

With a little gasp, eyes wide as she felt the strength of his arousal, she made one last plea for sanity. 'Henry…'

Ignoring her, he grasped a handful of her hair, tugged gently so that her face tilted upwards, and lowered his mouth to hers. Not gentle this time, but urgent, demanding, his own heart slamming against her own.

He kissed her with a passion he had never looked capable of. Shaped her back, her waist, her buttocks with warm palms, and, swept along on the tide of his need, of her own, she wrapped her arms around him, held him tight, kissed him back with a feverish intensity she had only ever dreamed of.

Hands roving, exploring, she encountered the edge of his black briefs, slid her thumbs inside, slowly eased them down as though she were an expert, used to doing this all the time, and she wasn't. 'Pretend we have been lovers for a very long time,' he'd said. And she wanted to. Wanted it to be familiar. Right.

Her gasp as the flesh of his arousal touched her jerked her mouth from his, shuddered the breath in her lungs, and he slid one hand to her nape, one to her buttocks, held her immobile, stared into her wide eyes. And the silence, the waiting, went on for a very long time. There was only the feel of him pressed against her, his warmth, the slight abrasion of his thighs against her own, and then he exerted the slightest of pressure against her buttocks, rubbed her against him.

'The world was made for this,' he stated thickly as he continued to stare at her, continued to hold her.

And she couldn't answer. Couldn't speak. Could only clench her hands tight on his shoulders, hang on. Mute.

He moved his hand from her nape to join the other, lifted her until her feet were clear of the floor, and settled her in a position against him that was unbelievably intimate.

Without instruction, without thought, hypnotised by silvery eyes, she lifted her legs and wrapped them round him. He eased himself inside her, and she gasped, held tight. 'Oh, Henry…'

'Yes,' he agreed. 'Now kiss me.'

Moving her eyes to his mouth, to lips that were

slightly parted, she groaned, touched her mouth to his, felt both their bodies react to this new sensation, this new closeness—and he gently lowered them onto the bed. Made love to her with a sweet aggression that nearly blew her mind.

Urgent, desperate, it was almost a fight to reach the ultimate peak, the final barrier; shaking with the intensity of it, they slumped together, held each other tight.

Eyes screwed shut, refusing to release him, she dragged long, deep breaths into her depleted lungs.

He moved, settled himself beside her, cradled her in his arms, blew softly against her closed lids.

'Githa…'

She frantically shook her head. Refused to look, answer, until he moved one palm slowly over her sensitised breasts, touched each hard peak in turn. Snapping open her eyes, she stared at him. He stared back.

'Don't ask me if I'm satisfied, will you?' he drawled.

She shook her head. Despaired. Without love, without affection, it seemed somehow degrading. He didn't love her any more than she loved him. It was just—carnal.

'Don't ask what happens now,' he continued in the same soft, slow voice. 'Because I intend to show you.' As he did.

She couldn't stop him, didn't want to stop him. Held captive by her body's needs. He could make her blood sing, arouse feelings she hadn't known she could feel. And she presumably did the same to him, because he didn't stop, didn't seem to want to stop. She had never known that lovemaking could go on for such a very long time. Had thought in her innocence that, once the deed was done, that was it. You made a cup of tea, or something. Talked. She hadn't known that you went *on*.

He touched her with gentleness, almost reverence, as he explored every inch of her, but it wasn't love that suffused his face. It was desire. An almost calculating absorption.

An incredibly competent lover, over the next two days he taught her to revel in experiences she had only ever read about. Like a drug, she began to need it more and more. And felt ashamed. Nice girls didn't make love with strangers, did they?

When he wasn't there—when he needed to return to the Hall to change, feed and exercise the dogs, catch up on the reading of manuscripts he'd brought with him—she could be rational, horrified by her behaviour. But when his absences went on too long she began to fidget, feel abandoned, empty. And she hated it. Hated this dependency. He commanded, however gently, and she obeyed. Willingly. Would he obey if she commanded? she wondered.

Slavish devotion, she thought bleakly, and she would *never* have believed she could be like that. There should be laughter and teasing and loving. But there wasn't. For all his involvement with her, part of him remained aloof. Separate. As did part of her, she supposed.

When he strolled into the kitchen a few minutes later, a half-smile on his face, a quizzical expression in his grey eyes, she stared at him somewhat assessingly.

He raised an eyebrow, waited.

'What is it you want from me, Henry?' she asked bluntly. 'Ultimately, I mean?'

Leaning his hips against the dresser behind him, he folded his arms across his chest, examined her face. 'I haven't considered it,' he replied equally bluntly. 'What is it you want from me?'

'I don't know,' she confessed. 'I don't even know if I *like* you. I don't know you, Henry.'

'Gloves off?' he asked softly. Righting himself, he walked across to the small table and sat down. 'Coffee?'

Automatically going towards the kettle, she suddenly stopped. 'No. *You* make it,' she said crossly. 'You command and I obey, and I don't *want* it like that!'

'And what is it that you do want?' he asked, still soft, still reasonable.

'I don't know!'

He smiled, got his feet, walked across to the kettle and switched it on.

'You didn't check if there was any water in it,' she muttered peevishly.

Slanting her a glance of pure mockery, he lifted the kettle, shook it, put it back.

With an irritated 'Hmph' she sat at the table, put her chin in her hands.

'Coffee?' he asked mildly.

'Yes.'

'Please,' he prompted.

'Please. Not too strong.'

He smiled, proceeded to make the coffee, and when it was ready he put hers before her, resumed his seat with his own cup and watched her across the table. 'Any more commands, Githa?'

'Not at the moment,' she said grumpily.

He watched her. Eyes still. 'You want a declaration of undying love?'

'No.'

'But you want to stop feeling—used, don't you?'

'Not *used* precisely,' she sighed. 'I just want to feel—valued. I feel a bit—degraded. As though I don't have a will of my own, a mind.'

'But you don't want me to stop making love to you, do you? That's the trouble, isn't it?'

Troubled, unhappy, she curved her hands round her mug, stared down, then lifted her eyes to his. 'Yes. There isn't any laughter, or teasing, or *happiness*, and it shouldn't be like that! Should it?'

'No,' he agreed. 'I've never seen you laugh, have I?'

'No,' she agreed quietly. 'I haven't seen you laugh, either.' In fact, she hadn't seen him do anything except confuse her, make love to her.

'I don't laugh much,' he said with gentle mockery. 'Tell me about the airline. About being a hostess. Handsome pilots.'

She gave a derisive snort.

'Your one lover was a pilot?'

She shook her head. 'Most of the pilots are married.'

'Which doesn't stop them having affairs.'

'No,' she agreed as she remembered one or two who had cheated quite blatantly on their wives. 'But we didn't generally mix with the pilots—not socially, anyway.'

'Never fancied any of them, Githa?'

'No,' she denied.

'And then you became famous, and they were a little afraid of you.'

Astonished, she just stared at him. 'Don't be absurd. All I did was front the airline's advertising campaign.'

'*All?* It was a golden opportunity to make your name.'

'Yes, but it didn't start out like that. It wasn't what I wanted, intended.'

'Wasn't it?' he asked with a touch of cynicism.

'No! You make it sound calculating, and it wasn't. It was all really rather accidental. They asked all the hostesses if any of them wanted to take a screen test, because they would prefer to have one of their own to advertise the airline rather than a paid model.'

'And so you took a test?' he mocked mildly. 'Were first in the queue?'

'No! I had no desire at all to model for them; I was quite happy doing what I was.' A little frown in her eyes, she said, 'You make me sound scheming, pushy, and I'm not like that. I don't particularly like being the centre of attention.'

'Then, if you didn't take a screen test, how did you end up becoming the airline's glamour girl?'

'Because I accidentally walked into the shot they were taking of the aircraft! I had no idea there was even a film crew in the vicinity!'

'Accidentally on purpose?'

'No! Why do you disbelieve me so readily? Do I *really* look that conniving?'

'No,' he admitted slowly, but he didn't sound entirely sure. 'And then?'

She shrugged. 'When they developed the film I was "discovered",' she said with an embarrassment she still felt. 'And when they met me in the flesh, compared me to myself on film, they thought it was just a fluke, and dismissed me. If they'd been able to find a model who was suitable, I would never have been remembered at all. But they couldn't find one, and so, probably in desperation, they filmed me again—again, when I wasn't aware of being filmed—and asked me to front their campaign. I refused. The big boss came to see me, persuaded me I had a duty to co-operate. And so I did.'

'And then the cosmetic giant saw the advertisement and wanted you for their face of the year.'

'Yes.'

'That simple, Githa?'

'Yes. You make it sound as though I should be ashamed, and I'm not. It was luck, pure and simple. Just being in the right place at the right time.'

'And being photogenic.'

'Yes.'

'And no grand passion with a pilot?'

'No. No grand passion. Not even a light flirtation. Matthew, my one lover, was someone I met at a party. We were together for a year. We fell out of love,' she added simply. Still feeling a bit defensive and cross, she asked bluntly, 'And you?'

'No, no grand passion. I don't think I even believed it existed—until I met you. And it is grand, isn't it, Githa?' he asked softly.

Blushing, she looked down, sighed. Yes, it was grand. 'The passion is,' she said quietly. 'But not the rest. I don't know what you like, dislike, how you think, feel. You keep yourself separate—and your upper-class drawl makes it sound as though you think yourself superior,' she grumbled.

'I do.'

Shocked, she just stared at him. 'What?'

'I do,' he repeated—and gave a slow, utterly mocking smile.

'Well, you aren't supposed to *admit* it!' she reproved.

He laughed. 'What an innocent you are, Githa.'

'I *know* I'm an innocent! I know I'm stupid and out of my depth!' And I want to be in love with you, she thought sadly, and I don't know *how*. I want it to be special and wonderful, and it isn't.

'And I've always been separate,' he murmured thoughtfully. 'I'm not a herd animal, Githa. Selfish? Arrogant? Probably. I don't *feel* things—not in a passionate way.' With a wry shrug, he leaned back, sipped his coffee. 'I don't like liars, or cheats…' With a half-laugh, he added, 'I don't like people much at all. I like my own company. Like my own thoughts. I've been fond of people, but I've never been in love. I'll help out a friend, but I won't be imposed upon. And I enjoy making love to you.'

'But you wouldn't be distraught if it ended, would you?' she asked bleakly. 'Wouldn't beg me to come back if I went away?'

Staring at her, watching her lovely face—the emotions, the sadness—he replied with quiet honesty, 'No, I wouldn't beg. Would you, Githa?'

'No. I don't think I'm a begging sort of person.' But I would miss you. And I would ache. Always wonder if there might have been more. 'For it to work,' she murmured sadly, 'I think you have to be in love.'

'And you aren't in love with me, are you?' he asked gently.

'No. I find you attractive, you make my heart race, make me feel breathless and wanting. If you touch me, I melt. But that isn't love, is it?'

He stared down into his coffee and replaced the mug on the table. 'You want me to go away?'

'No,' she denied helplessly. 'I want to know how to fall in love with you. How to make you fall in love with me.'

'And then everything would be all right?'

With a funny little smile, she shook her head. 'I

don't know. Perhaps I think too much. *Want* too much.'

'Which is better than wanting too little.'

'Yes.' Looking across at him, staring into eyes that didn't communicate, she felt need and want stir inside. That helpless yearning that seemed never to be assuaged. 'Make love to me, Henry.'

His eyes darkened, glittered, and he gave a twisted smile. 'Because I have my uses?'

'No, because… It's all we seem to have. It doesn't matter.' Getting abruptly to her feet, she turned away. He rose, caught her, swung her round to face him, and into his arms. Hard into his arms.

CHAPTER THREE

'HERE? Now? On the kitchen floor?' Henry asked brutally.

Suddenly frightened because he looked so dangerously sexy, a stranger, she shook her head, and her eyes pleaded with him.

He ignored her, tugged her off balance, laid her on the cold tiles, lay above her. He undid her shirt, knocked her hands aside when she tried to stop him, exposed her breasts to his gaze.

'Henry, don't!'

'Yes.' Bending his head, he touched his mouth to hers, sought for a response—and found it. Excited, hot, aching, ashamed, she kissed him back, held him tight, allowed him to do all that he wanted to do. Allowed him to destroy what little peace of mind she had left. He used his tongue, his hands, even the silkiness of his hair to arouse her. And when she was almost sobbing with frustration, begging, he gently punished her for her arrogance.

Lying above her, his weight supported on his elbows, he spread her dark curly hair out over the cold tiles, stared down into her flushed face. 'You want me to apologise?' he asked quietly.

She gave a weak shake of her head.

'No,' he agreed, 'because it's what you wanted.

What we both wanted. I excite you. You excite me. And *that*'s what comes through on camera. Your sensuality, your sex. The *you* hidden inside. The *you* you won't let out because it frightens you. It isn't me who frightens you, Githa, it's you—and you're afraid to let her out in case she swamps you.'

'No.'

'Yes. There's a glorious, uninhibited being trapped inside, and she wants out, wants to be free. You can't revel in our lovemaking, can you? Because part of you feels guilty, ashamed, and so you insist there must be more. Enjoy it, Githa,' he said dismissively. 'Revel in it. Not many people feel what you feel. Express it. Tell the world.'

'You won't.'

'No, but neither will I repress it, make excuses for it.'

'But you're a man. It's expected of men. It's not expected of women.'

'Rubbish. I'm not telling you to be promiscuous, to sleep with any man who asks. I'm telling you to enjoy what you have. To stop feeling guilty for enjoying, wanting a pleasure as old as time.'

'With you.'

'Yes. With me.'

For now.

'You're so—dispassionate!' she exclaimed. 'Don't you feel *anything* for me?'

'Yes. Desire.'

And then, quite suddenly, he relaxed, all the anger

gone. And he smiled. A quirky, amused, attractive smile. A smile she had not seen before.

I could love you, she told him silently. I *could*. If you would share with me—thoughts, feelings. But he wouldn't. And she was afraid to love him, wasn't she? Because he didn't seem the sort of man who would ever love her back. Elegant, intense, complicated. Aloof. The sort of man who always belonged to someone else.

'Your parents died when you were a baby, didn't they?'

Cautious, wary, not knowing where this was leading, she nodded.

'Like Lucinda's. And you were brought up by an aunt?'

'Yes.'

'Was she religious?'

'Religious? No, not particularly.'

'A spinster?'

'Yes, but…'

'Very moral? *Was* she, Githa?'

Turning her head away, she stared at the wall. 'Yes.'

'And so you feel guilty, because all of this—enjoyment—is outside the sanctity of marriage. Did you feel guilty with your one lover?'

'No,' she replied stiffly.

'Because you thought yourself in love with him?' he asked, more gently.

Turning back to face him, she searched his face, reluctantly nodded.

'But you aren't in love with me, and so Little Githa's hang-ups have all surfaced.'

'"Little Githa" does not *have* hang-ups. "Little Githa" has…' Yes? What did Little Githa have?

'Hang-ups,' he said softly. 'It is allowed to enjoy sex. You aren't selling yourself short. Being cheap.'

'Aren't I?'

'No. It's repression that's unhealthy.'

'I'm not repressed!'

'No, just unhappy. Let go of the worries, Githa. Enjoy.'

'The way you do? Without feeling? Without liking?'

'Don't be a fool.'

A fool? Did that mean he did have feeling? Liking? Searching his eyes, she asked with hope, 'Do you? Have feeling for me?'

'Of course. I wonder why it never occurred to me that you might be vulnerable, insecure. Because you are, aren't you?'

'Only with you, I think.'

'On camera you look sophisticated, alluring, and your eyes hint at exciting possibilities. Off camera you can look elegant, worldly, as though you know all about—games.'

'Is this what this is? A game?' she asked sadly.

He smiled again, shook his head. 'A glorious desire. And since you've been here,' he continued, 'you've looked like a tomboy, someone fun to be with.'

She sighed. 'I used to be fun to be with. But these last few months…'

'Have been a strain. A worry. But you're young, healthy, and words, gestures, are only that. You haven't been physically attacked, only mentally, so stop looking so tragic. He can only hurt you if you let him.'

The way Henry could only hurt her if she let him? With a tiny smile, she murmured wryly, 'In other words, "Don't whinge"?'

'Yes.'

'It isn't you he's doing it to!'

'No,' he agreed. 'And, as for us, enjoy what we have together. Make the most of it. Experience enriches the soul,' he mocked. 'One day you'll no doubt be married, with babies, and you can look back and—smile.'

Was that what he did? Looked back and smiled?

He waited, watched, whilst she thought about it, and then she sighed, raised one hand to gently trace his aristocratic features. 'And you won't ever be married with babies?'

His eyes amused, he shook his head.

'No,' she agreed. 'You don't look like husband material—father material—but then,' she murmured, 'you don't look like a man who would want to romp on the floor.'

'Don't I? What *do* men who want to romp on the floor look like? And that's the first time you've touched me voluntarily.'

'Is it?' she asked almost absently as she continued

to trace his face, and then she slipped her fingers into his silky hair, revelled in the feel of it against her palm.

'Henry?'

'Yes?'

'Do you hate it?'

'Hate it?'

'This feeling of being out of control. Because you feel it too, don't you? You don't like me, don't want this to be happening, but—' Breaking off, she sighed.

'Is that how you feel?'

'Sometimes. No, not sometimes,' she confessed honestly, 'all the time. I want you, want to keep touching you, but I do feel used.'

'And you think I don't?'

Eyes widening in surprise, she asked, 'You?'

'Of course. It works both ways. And, yes, I sometimes hate it. I go away, and I think, That's it, I will finish it. It's only a woman, and women are a complication I don't need—but my body seems to think differently.'

'Slaves to our bodies' needs.' A sudden smile in her eyes—the first time she had ever really smiled at him—she approved, 'And you do have a nice body.'

A little quirk to his mouth, he queried humorously, 'Do I?'

'Yes. Stronger than you look. I mean, you held me up that first time… What did he want? Whoever it was who called you by the woodpile.'

'Max? One of my neighbours. He wanted to ask

me about my car. He's thinking of buying one the same.'

'Oh.'

'Any more questions? Only this floor seems to be getting harder by the second.'

'It's called conversation. We don't have those, do we?' she asked wistfully.

'Don't we?'

'No.'

'Then, if we must have one, do you think we could have it in bed? I'm not at all enamoured of this cold floor, nor of having my clothes tangled around me like a schoolboy on his first fumble.'

She grinned, her eyes amused. 'I can't imagine you as a fumbling schoolboy.'

'Can't you?'

'No, you're much too elegant and assured.'

'Well, I don't look very elegant at the moment, nor do I feel very assured—or was that the plan?'

She shook her head. 'I didn't want to move because I like the feel of you against me.'

'I feel much better in a bed,' he said firmly. Levering himself upright, he adjusted what clothing he had left, hoisted her to her feet, and propelled her upstairs.

'Have you ever stayed here before?' she asked, with what she hoped was casual interest.

'No.'

'Never?'

'No.'

'You and Cindy weren't...?'

'No.' Pushing her gently onto the bed, he lay beside her, propped his head up on his hand, stared mockingly into her innocent face.

'Just asking.' Rolling onto her tummy, supporting herself on her forearms, she stared at him. An almost clinical appraisal. 'I think I'm going to pretend I'm in love with you,' she stated recklessly.

'Are you? Why?'

'Because then I would have the right to touch you, kiss you, and not feel as though it was something you might not want me to do.'

'Is that how I make you feel?'

'Yes. A bit intimidated. You don't at all look like the sort of man I might have an affair with, you see.'

'I don't?'

'No. You're elegant and fastidious, and I'm a bit of a heap sometimes.'

Eyes amused, he continued to watch her.

'And I know on the commercials and films I look as though I'm in charge of my life, but I'm not really like that.'

'No,' he agreed. 'Not at all sophisticated, are you, Githa?'

'No. So, shall you?'

'Shall I what?'

'Mind if I touch you?'

Eyes a little bit darker, body slowing, he said with a slight huskiness to his voice, 'No, Githa, I shan't mind if you touch me. I'm sorry if I gave the impression that everything had to be on my terms. I don't always consider people's feelings. Or so I've been accused,' he added wryly.

'That's all right; I expect you didn't know how I felt.'

'No. So please touch me, because I'm beginning to feel extraordinarily light-headed.'

Her own body warming, becoming heavy, languid, her eyes on his, she whispered, 'Are you?'

'Yes,' he agreed thickly. 'And although they say it's often better to travel than to arrive I don't altogether agree with that precept. Or not right at this moment. Anticipation is playing the very devil with my hormones.'

Leaning closer, so that her breasts brushed against his chest, she touched a tongue to his nipple, shivered at the small quiver he gave, and whispered faintly, 'You speak so nicely.'

'I won't be speaking nicely in a moment,' he managed, with a slight edge to his voice, 'if you don't get on with it...'

Flicking her eyes up to his, she grinned. 'Don't like being tantalised?'

'I think the word is "tormented", and, no, I don't. So either touch, or take the consequences, Miss James.'

With a sly smile, she pushed one hand beneath the duvet, slid it across his flat stomach, moved it lower, felt his muscles contract.

'Power,' she murmured gleefully. 'No! Don't!' she warned when he grabbed her. 'You have to lie still.'

'Impossible.' Levering her over onto her back, he

straddled her, held her arms out to the sides. 'Now who has power?'

'That's not fair. You're stronger than me.'

He shook his head. 'No, Milgitha, I really don't think I am.' Bending forward, he touched his mouth to hers, kissed her until she squirmed for release, the chance to reciprocate, but he held her wrists immobile, used his knees to restrain her arching body, and kissed her and kissed her until she felt faint.

'Did I hurt you?' He sounded shaken.

She shook her head. 'I shall have to remember in the future not to tease you.'

'No,' he groaned, 'don't remember that.' Rolling to the side, he pulled her on top of him, gently soothed her wrists, held them to his mouth. Eyes serious, he repeated, 'Don't remember that. I don't ever recall losing control. You were right, Githa, you have a great deal of power.'

'No!' Upset, hurt that she might have hurt him with careless words, she whispered, 'No, I don't want to have power. I just want to be happy. To smile with you, laugh. Don't make me have power over you, Henry. Please don't.'

Puzzled, he stared at her, and then gently drew her against him, cuddled her as he had never cuddled her before. Ran his palms soothingly up and down her back. 'You say you don't understand me—and now I don't understand you. I thought…' With a long sigh, he continued, 'You aren't at all as I imagined you. I saw you, I wanted you, and I rather foolishly thought that you were like me.'

'Like you? In what way like you?'

'Unemotional.'

'But you aren't!' she protested.

'Yes, Githa, I am.'

Troubled, she raised her head, stared into his face—a face that no longer looked superior, arrogant, but really rather brooding.

'I envisaged a rather loose arrangement—I would come and see you when I had time. You would welcome me with the same—need. A mutual—necessity, if you like. But when I spoke to you in the studio, saw your bewilderment and vulnerability, I knew that I had the power to hurt you. I don't normally play with innocents, Githa. Only those that know the rules. Are—experienced in the ways of the world. I assumed you would be like that. And you aren't. But I found that I didn't want to walk away. I should have done. But I didn't want to.'

'But surely Cindy told you what I was like?'

'Yes,' he agreed slowly, 'but I obviously misinterpreted her words.'

'Misinterpreted? How?'

'Oh, I don't know...'

'Yes, you do! Downstairs, earlier, you thought I was mercenary, pushy—surely Cindy didn't tell you that?' she stated in hurt surprise.

'No-o,' he denied slowly, 'but...' A slight frown in his eyes, he added, 'But I suspect that my experience of women rather coloured what she said. I expected you to be like that, and so I assumed that you were.'

'But you still came to see me,' she whispered.

'Yes. Stared into wide green eyes, and was lost.'

'Hazel,' she corrected absently.

'Green,' he insisted. 'Eyes of a witch. But I didn't want to *know* you. Not as a person. Neither did I wish to hurt you. There are no deep *feelings* here, Githa, just a general liking, an amusement. And a devouring desire,' he added, almost too softly to be heard.

Eyes locked, that warm helplessness overcame her again, that need to touch and be touched. Moving her eyes to his mouth, she leaned nearer, nearer, until she could touch, taste. Gave a helpless little groan as she felt his body respond. Wanted to make slow, gentle love to him, make everything be nice, because it sounded as though he was going to leave, didn't it? And she desperately didn't want him to.

Moving into a more comfortable position, a more accommodating position, she slid her hands to his throat, touched her mouth once more to his, touched her tongue to his lips, and began to make love to him as she wanted to be loved—with gentleness, enjoyment, and a lasting fulfilment. It felt as though it could go on for ever. Should go on for ever. And he was gentle. Incredibly gentle. Almost loving.

Cuddled warmly beside him, mouth against his chest, she murmured on a rather sad sigh, 'That was beautiful.'

'Yes, it was. Thank you.'

'You're welcome.' And he laughed. It sounded genuine. It almost sounded happy. Perhaps he was right. Let go of the worries and just—enjoy. But she knew his words would stay with her. A testament to their differences.

Smoothing one hand over her hair, he said quietly, 'Be patient with me, Githa. This is a whole new departure for me.'

'This isn't the end?' She looked up with surprise.

'End?'

'I thought you were saying—goodbye,' she finished painfully.

He searched her eyes, then tucked her head back beneath his chin. 'No.'

Silent for a moment, she finally asked, 'Have your experiences with women been so very terrible?'

'Terrible? No.'

'But they weren't like this?'

'No. The women weren't like you. They didn't expect anything—emotional.'

'Just rewards for favours given?' she guessed.

'Yes. Presents, jewellery, expensive wining and dining. But you aren't like that, are you, Githa?'

'No. It's hard enough coping with my feelings, without being bought and paid for. There doesn't seem to be a choice about this. I don't even know if I would like to have one. It's new for me too, Henry.'

'I know. Now.' With a lazy smile, a gentle kiss on her hair, he murmured, 'But I will have to make a move.'

'Move?'

'Mmm. I have to go back to London. Work to do. People to see. Places to go.'

'When will you be back?'

'Late. Or early tomorrow.'

Because of the dogs. Reluctant to move, feeling sleepy and warm, happier now that she knew he would be coming back, she idly traced his ribs. 'Drive safely.'

'Mmm. Don't go to sleep.'

'No.' But her eyelids were heavy, her body comfortable, warm, and so she snuggled against him, let her eyelids drop, and drifted into sleep to dream of permanence, of happy endings…

When she woke it was dark, and Henry had gone. Stretching, yawning, she lay for a while, remembering, and then smiled. Perhaps it would be all right. For the first time since she'd met him, it *felt* all right.

She got up, had something to eat, and went back to bed at gone midnight to sleep deeply, dreamlessly, until after eight the following morning.

She breakfasted in the kitchen, went for her usual walk, to drag back any branches she found for the fire—and then everything changed. The nightmare came back.

Kicking off her muddy trainers, she padded through the back door, and stared frowningly at the thick envelope lying in the centre of the kitchen table. Half assumed Henry must have left it.

Picking it up, she undid the flap and tipped out the contents. Photographs. Still puzzled, curious, she picked them up and began to look through them—and curiosity turned to disgust, fear, because they were all of her, taken here. The last few days she'd almost forgotten about the stalker, about being persecuted…

Photographs of her leaving the Hall… Photographs of her undressing in her bedroom… And there were pin-holes in her eyes, her heart, she saw. He had deliberately and maliciously… With an angry, frightened little cry, she hurled them at the wall—just as Henry walked in.

CHAPTER FOUR

'You told someone,' Githa accused him tightly.

'No.'

'Then Cindy must have. Yet why would she?' she frowned. 'That was the whole point of her lending me the cottage—so that no one would know where I was!'

'Maybe she didn't. Maybe he followed you here,' said Henry, quietly, reasonably. 'Did you check your mirrors when you were driving up?'

'No.'

He didn't say anything else, but she heard him pick up the scattered photographs and presumably look at them, before he walked to the table and fitted them carefully inside the envelope.

'Not professionally processed,' he commented. 'But then, it's easy enough to get all the equipment to develop your own. And no negatives,' he added quietly.

She didn't answer.

'How did they come?'

'They were on the table when I came in,' she said flatly. 'Which means he was here in the cottage. Which means he—' Breaking off, she slammed her hand against the window sill. 'He could have...'

'But didn't.'

'No. But he's out there, isn't he? Waiting, watching. And now it's all spoilt. *Why?*' Swinging round, she glared at him. 'Why?' she whispered.

'I don't know.'

'And he put holes through my eyes...' Voice cracking, she swung away, and Henry walked across to her, pulled her gently into his arms.

'How did he get in?'

'In?' she echoed, her voice muffled against her sweater. Lifting her head, she stared vaguely round her, as though seeking inspiration.

'You've been out?'

'Yes, just up into the woods, looking for branches for the fire.'

'You locked up?'

Had she? 'No,' she confessed.

He glanced at the envelope. 'You want me to destroy them?'

'No. The police said to keep everything I get for evidence,' she said bitterly, 'in case they catch the bastard.'

'And this all started when you were employed by Varlane?'

'Don't *interrogate* me, Henry!' Shoving him away, she returned to stand at the window, her back to him.

'Did it?' he insisted, without change of inflexion.

'Yes!' she bit out.

'And have you thought that it might be a woman? Someone who didn't get the job? Someone who wanted it very badly?'

'Of course I've thought about it! I've thought of

very little else for the past three months! But Varlane checked out all the applicants—couldn't find anything—suspicious.'

Eyes thoughtful, he ordered quietly, 'Get packed up; I'll go and take a look around.'

'Don't *order* me, Henry!'

He halted, looked back at her. Waited.

'Sorry,' she muttered. 'I'm *angry*. And I'm not running away.'

'You can't stay here.'

'Of course I can stay here! I'll…'

'What? Find him? Confront him?'

'Stop being so *reasonable*!'

Walking across to her, he gently touched her face with his long fingers. 'You can't stay here,' he repeated softly. 'I can't be with you all the time.'

'I don't want you with me all the time!'

'Githa…'

Swinging away, she muttered defiantly, 'He won't hurt me.'

'Won't he?'

Eyes wide, frightened, she wanted to weep. 'It could even be you,' she said without conviction.

'Could,' he agreed quietly. 'But isn't.'

'I mean, you erupted into my life without warning. Came up here… I don't know what to *do* any more, Henry!'

'But I do. Go and pack your things.' He waited, watched, and she finally slumped, nodded.

'It isn't fair!'

'No,' he agreed, and walked out.

'Don't go far!' she called after him, and heard him call back that he wouldn't.

Standing where he had left her, she stared at the envelope on the table. Snatching it up, she looked through the photographs again, tried to identify when each had been taken. Until she came to a particular one—almost a full frontal, obviously taken through the landing window as she'd padded naked out of the bathroom. A morning shot, because a weak sunlight was gilding her body. Face twisting, she ripped it to shreds. *That* wasn't ever going to be shown in any evidence! No one was ever going to snigger over *that*!

Feeling suddenly sick, shaken despite her bravado, she gathered them all up again, shoved them into the envelope. Why hadn't Henry *seen* anything when she'd left the Hall? He'd been out with the dogs! Surely he must have seen something? Or the animals. Dogs were supposed to investigate anything suspicious, weren't they?

Taking the photographs out again, almost as though it was a compulsion, as though they might change, become *holiday* snaps, she stared at them. They'd been taken from high up—her back view as she walked along the track. From a tree, maybe? Was that why no one had seen him?

Slamming them down, fists clenched, she stared at nothing. She felt—abused. And where were the negatives? What were they to be used for? Was he watching her still? Seeing her reaction?

'Well, make the bloody most of it!' she yelled, but her voice broke on a sob. Teeth gritted, refusing to cry, she marched defiantly upstairs to pack. But first she drew all the curtains. She packed with speed, in case...

That was what angered her—this curtailment of her privacy. At least he didn't have any shots of her with Henry... Or did he? Were they to be the next 'gift'? Or was it because Henry had taken them? An errant thought, but... No. Don't be absurd, Githa. Henry doesn't need to send you *pictures*.

When he returned, she was ready, waiting. Angry.

'Nothing?' she asked quietly.

He shook his head, eyes sombre as they rested on her.

'And you didn't see *anything* when I left the Hall the other day?'

'No.'

'Bloody good dogs you've got if they can't even find an *intruder*!'

'Yes,' he agreed. 'Fridge off? Dishwasher door open?'

'Yes,' she agreed stiffly. 'I've locked the back door, the windows.'

He nodded, picked up her suitcase, waited whilst she picked up the box of groceries, and led the way out. He set the alarm, closed and locked the front door, and carried her case to her car.

'You know the number,' she said quietly.

'Sorry?'

'The alarm number.'

He stopped, looked at her, then explained patiently, 'Of course I know the number. We keep a check on the cottage when Cindy's not here. You want me to drive?'

She gave a listless nod. 'Sorry. What about your car?'

He glanced at her, puzzled. 'What about it?'

Exasperated, she snapped, 'Well, it will be up here and you'll be down there!'

'Down where?'

'London!'

'We aren't going to London,' he informed her as he put her case and the groceries in the boot.

'Then where are we going?'

'The Hall.'

'The *Hall*? *Your* Hall?'

'Of course my Hall. Get in the car, Githa.'

'No. And we can't go to the Hall. You don't want me there; you want a loose arrangement. You said so! And we can hardly have a loose arrangement when I'm living in your house.'

With a sigh, he walked round the car, opened the passenger door, pushed her in. 'Do up your belt.'

'Henry!'

He walked back, climbed behind the wheel, and fired the engine.

He drove down the track to the road, turned left, then left again when he came to another entrance, and all the while she searched the tree line, the fields, each car that passed. Felt mutinous, unsettled, angry.

'Used to be a carriage drive,' he murmured. 'Wrought-iron gates. Deer park.'

'What did?'

'This. Pay attention, Githa.'

'I was looking for…'

'I know.'

Turning to look at him, and then at the track, the sheep in the field, she sighed. 'Deer park?'

'Yes.'

'And now it's all gone?'

'Yes. Over the centuries, whenever the resident family needed money—which was often—the land was sold off bit by bit, until only Blakeborough Hall remained.'

'Blakeborough?'

'Mmm. Miles Blakeborough was the original owner.' He removed a hand from the wheel, squeezed hers where it lay on her lap. 'Don't give in,' he urged softly.

'No.' But how much longer was it to go on for? For ever? 'Won't your family mind me staying here?'

'No.'

'When will they be back?'

'A few days.'

She sighed, stared at the approaching Hall. From the front it looked even more dilapidated than the rear, but really rather comforting. It had stood for a very long time—seen riot, strife, civil war—and here it still was. A testament to—endurance.

'And this is where Cindy used to pop in and out?'

'Still pops in and out,' he corrected.

'I didn't know,' she murmured indifferently. 'That this was where she grew up.' Funny, that. They'd been friends for such a long time, and she had never known where Cindy had been brought up.

He drove through an arch, parked by the stable block that housed the tractor.

'Why do you need a tractor?' she asked quietly.

'Tom uses it to drag in logs for the fire. Uses it as an off-roader,' he smiled. 'Careers through the woods like Indiana Jones on a mission.'

'Your stepfather?'

'Yes.'

'You like him?'

'Very much.' Switching off the engine, he turned towards her, examined her sad face. 'Think of the very worst thing he can do to you,' he said quietly, 'and then think how you would deal with it. He's a coward, Githa. You're not.'

'It's only anger that's sustaining me,' she confessed miserably.

'Then stay angry.'

'And when I think that he's been watching me, has seen me...'

'Then don't think,' he advised.

'But it's all so *pointless*!'

'No, it isn't. It's hurting you, frightening you, and that's what he wants.'

'But I don't know *why*. And I need to.'

'There might not be a reason—not one that's logical to you or me. Maybe he just saw you, and for whatever reason—a grudge, an obsession, or a sick mind—he needs to act out this—fantasy. You said you got letters. What did they say?'

With a long sigh she leaned back, stared up at the trees. 'Is he up there now, do you suppose?'

'Maybe. What did the letters say?'

'That I was a bitch, that I deserved all I got— Oh, I don't know,' she despaired wearily. 'Just generally reviled me.'

'But didn't specifically threaten you?'

'No, just letters, words cut out of a newspaper. Sometimes they didn't even make sense. But hatred came through. In whatever he writes, it always seems full of hate. And that's what frightens me. Whatever did I do to make someone hate me so much? I've thought and *thought*...'

Tilting her face towards him, he kissed her gently on the mouth. 'Don't start blaming yourself for someone else's problem. Come on, let's get you inside.'

The dogs were lined up as before, looking equally guilty, and she gave a shaky smile. Dumping the box of groceries on the kitchen table, she bent to ruffle their ears, then looked round her. She hadn't really noticed much before, just the old range, the pine table and chairs, the cheerful curtains. The late April sun felt warm through the windows. Welcoming.

'Leave the box there; I'll show you up to my room.'

'Yours?' she asked softly, and he halted, looked at her from beneath his lids.

'You'd prefer one of your own?'

She shrugged. 'I don't know. Your family might not like...'

'Me having a resident mistress? I'm sure they'll be ecstatic,' he mocked obscurely. 'Come on.'

Following him up the wide, very worn staircase, she felt—helpless, as though she was incapable of making any decisions of her own. And that just wasn't like her.

He led her along to the back of the house, past old portraits, numerous doors, another passageway, and halted before an old oak door at the end. He glanced at her, gave a faint, enigmatic smile, then pushed it open—and she gasped. The room was enormous—like a state apartment—and it was dominated by a four-poster bed draped in dark red brocade, gold tassels. She stared at it in shock.

'Charles the First stayed here, right?'

He shook his head, walked inside and put her case by the bed.

'Cavaliers? Marauding Roundheads?'

'Not to my knowledge, but entirely possible. We do have a priest's hole.'

'Naturally. Dungeons?'

'A cellar,' he said apologetically.

Glancing at him, then back to the enormous bed, she smiled, then laughed. 'Oh, Henry.'

'Mmm.'

Two sets of high, wide mullioned windows, window seats, and wooden shutters that closed from the inside. A writing desk—antique by the look of it— two squashy armchairs either side of an enormous fireplace, and a tasselled bell-pull.

Still smiling, still delighted, she walked across to it, glanced at Henry in query. 'Does it work?'

'No. The wires broke a long, long time ago.'

'Shame. No family retainer?'

'No family retainer,' he agreed.

Turning, her back to the fireplace, she stared at the rest of the room. 'It's wonderful.'

'Yes.'

'And will it all be yours one day?'

'Mmm.'

'Then I think you ought to marry me. I would *love* to be chatelaine of all this.'

'Would you?'

'Yes.'

'The roof leaks.'

'Oh.'

'The drains need replacing, the walls repainting, it's freezing in winter, freezing in summer…'

'And you don't want a wife,' she stated mournfully.

'No.'

A little smile in her eyes, she walked across to him and slid her arms round his neck. 'Then I'd best settle for mistress, hadn't I?'

'Yes.'

Pulling her against him, settling her comfortably against his long frame, he stared down into her lovely face. Gently kissed her.

'Why did you bring me here?'

'You know why.'

'Yes, but you said…'

'Of others. Not of you. I also said you were to enjoy it. Revel in it, and so I intend to see that you do. But first we have to take the dogs out.'

'Do we?'

'Yes. I didn't have time when I got back.'

'Didn't you?'

'No.' His eyes crinkled at the corners. 'Too eager to see you, I expect. I missed you.'

'Did you? That's nice.'

'Mmm. And Mother will kill me if they look neglected.'

'Afraid of her, are you?'

'Terrified.'

'Where is she?'

'Scotland. An opportunity to meet up with an old friend.'

'And she asked you to come and look after them?'

'Mmm.'

'Convenient timing, just when I was staying at the cottage,' she murmured with a teasing smile.

'Mmm.'

'You encouraged your mother to go for these particular days?'

'Mmm.'

'Wasn't she suspicious?'

'My mother is always suspicious.'

'Oh, dear.' Lowering her long lashes, she stared at his shirt, gave a slow grin. 'And if Cindy hadn't lent me the cottage?'

'We would have stayed in London.'

Nestling more comfortably against him, she murmured without much interest, 'I don't even know their names.'

'Whose names?'

'The dogs'!'

'Ah. Ben and Luther.'

Glancing up, feeling warm and safe, excited, she thought about it. 'Luther's the Alsation?'

'Mmm.'

'For—Martin Luther King?'

'Clever girl.'

'Because he's…?'

'Black, obviously, and because he's strong, full of integrity, honesty, and extraordinarily loyal.'

'Who named him?'

'Mother. She said he looked like a leader. It was either that or Othello, but Tom utterly refused to yell ''Othello'' out of the back door.'

'Do we have to go now?' she asked softly.

Amusement leaked into his eyes. Amusement and something else. 'Oh,' he drawled, 'I don't think five minutes one way or the other will matter too much.'

'I was intending more than five minutes.'

'Were you?'

'Mmm.' Sliding her hands to his nape, she slowly kissed him—until a kiss was no longer enough. As kisses were never enough.

'Draw the curtains,' she whispered raggedly against his mouth.

'No need,' he told her, his voice as uneven as hers. Lifting her, he laid her on the bed, tugged a gold tassel, and the curtains enfolded them.

'And now I can't see you,' he murmured as his mouth traversed her cheek, her jaw, moved down to her warm neck. His hand began to undo buttons, slide across her ribs.

'Touch is nice.'

'Yes,' he said against her shoulder. 'Tactile, erotic.'

'Warm and safe in the dark.'

She undressed him, as he undressed her, with slow pleasure, until breathing was restricted, until they were naked, and warm flesh could slide against warm flesh. And in the dark it was easier to be—innovative, to shed inhibitions—be someone else. Someone erotic and sexy and bold.

The most magical experience of her life. Because he couldn't see her, read the expressions on her face.

And when they lay, warmly entwined, waiting for their breathing to return to normal, neither spoke; they just breathed as one. She didn't know what he was thinking—only knew what she was wishing. For time to stop, to remain cocooned in this warmth with a man who made life special, exciting—sad. I could love you, she told him silently. I could.

Carefully moving her head, she stared at his shadowed face, gently lifted one hand to trace her forefinger against his mouth. He parted it, bit gently on the nail. And excitement flowed through her again, that shivery feeling of need, want, desire.

'Henry,' she whispered on a groan, and he turned, rolled to cover her, kissed her with an urgency that was echoed in her mind, her body. Parting her thighs, she allowed him inside again, matched his growing demand with demands of her own, held him tight. Almost desperately so. Revelled aggressively in a pleasure as old as time. And when it was over, when both were weak, aching, he pulled the bed curtains back.

'Someone might see.'

'*I* want to see.'

'Do you?' she asked thickly.

'Yes. And unless he's in a helicopter, hovering outside the window, it's quite impossible for anyone to see into this room, see anyone on this bed.'

Kneeling up, he stroked his palms slowly down her body, watched her shiver with awareness, and it excited him. He probed intimate places with his thumbs. 'We could be here all day,' he said thickly.

'Yes,' she agreed, her own voice a mere whisper of sound. 'Henry… Oh, dear God, Henry.' Muscles clenched tight, she groaned, arched her back. 'I didn't know I could… So many times…' With a last little cry, she curled away, held her own body close, fought to breathe—and he still didn't stop.

'Henry, no,' she pleaded weakly.

'Yes.'

'No.' Grabbing him, she pulled him off balance, held his hands still across his chest, stared into his face. His eyes were a dark, slumberous grey, his mouth slightly parted as though breathing might be a problem. And it excited her, so then it was she who touched, made him gasp, made him—satisfied.

With hands that shook slightly, he held the hair back from her face, stared at her exquisite bone structure. Breathing still slightly laboured, he asked huskily, 'No more guilt?'

She shook her head. But there was a growing need to be loved.

'Shower?'

'Together?' she rasped.

'Mmm.'

'Don't you think that might be—dangerous?'

'Who wants to be safe?'

'This is madness.'

'Yes, but I find that I don't want the madness to end.'

But it would, wouldn't it? One day it would end. 'I don't think I can move.'

He smiled. Proved that she could.

When they'd showered, and whilst she was dressing—well away from the window—Henry asked to look through the photographs again.

'Because?'

'I want to identify where they were taken from.'

Taking them out of her case, she handed them to him. 'Get dressed first.'

'In a minute,' he murmured absently as he flicked through them. 'There's one missing.'

'Yes,' she agreed, giving him a defiant look.

'You destroyed it?'

'Yes.'

He merely nodded. Getting to his feet, unashamedly naked, he walked to the window, the photographs held in his hand.

Long, shapely back, long legs, broad shoulders and narrow waist. Beautifully slender. Well muscled. And, despite the slight chill in the room, his skin looked warm, eminently touchable.

'The ones of you leaving the Hall were taken from up high.'

'Yes,' she agreed as she joined him at the window, scanned the trees ahead of them.

'From this angle, or near to it.'

'Mmm.' Resting one hand against his naked back, she stared over his shoulder at the top photograph, then moved her eyes to the track she had taken that day. But her mind wasn't really on the view; it was more taken up with the feel of his warm flesh beneath her hand. Resting her cheek against him, she touched her mouth to his shoulder.

'Behave,' he ordered mildly.

'Don't want to.'

He slanted her a glance of pure mockery, handed her the photographs, and went to get dressed.

She sighed, stared out at the view. 'That tree by the window, do you think?'

'Possible,' he murmured from behind her. 'And put a sweater on; it's cold out.'

With an absent nod, she returned the photographs to the envelope and went to get a sweater from her suitcase.

'We'll take the dogs out, then go into Ludlow to have something to eat.'

'OK.'

He gave a small grin. 'You're very obedient all of a sudden.'

'I'm always obedient. I'm a very acquiescent lady.'

'Yes,' he agreed softly, and she blushed.

'I didn't mean—that!'

'Didn't you? Come on, I'm hungry. Neither of us had any lunch.'

'I have to put sun-block on.'

'Githa, there's barely any sun!'

'But there is wind, and pollution.' Borrowing some of his mockery, she gazed at him with smiling derision. 'And beautiful skins have to be protected. It's in the contract,' she added softly, and he gave a wry smile.

'Then protect it quickly.'

Before setting out, Henry walked over to look at the tree that grew beside his bedroom window. Looked for marks, signs that someone might have been there, climbed it.

'Nothing?'

'No.'

'I suppose I ought to inform the local police...'

'Already done. I rang from the farm when I was out looking. I also asked John to report any strangers he might see.'

'Oh. Thank you.'

'Come on.'

They took the dogs for their run, then drove into Ludlow just as it was getting dark.

Parking behind the supermarket, they walked along the high street. 'We'll eat in The Feathers.'

She smiled. 'Will we? The Feathers being...?' she queried humorously.

He pointed towards a seventeenth-century inn. 'You haven't been doing your research, Miss James. I would have expected...'

'Mr Sheldrake!'

They halted, looked round, waited whilst a young man rushed breathlessly up to them.

'Mr Sheldrake?'

'Yes,' he agreed, with a cold reserve that rather shook Githa. He hadn't been like that since the day in the studio.

'I've written a book...'

'Send it into the office,' he said dismissively. Taking Githa's arm again, he turned her back in the direction of the hotel.

'But I have it here!'

Henry ignored him.

'Mr Sheldrake!'

He halted, turned, stared at the young man with thinning brown hair and an anxious face.

'You'll like it. It's good.'

'Then what a pity I shan't have a chance to read it,' he drawled.

'What?'

'I dislike being accosted in the street. I dislike being argued with. And I very much dislike people who refuse to obey instructions. I asked you to send it to the office—I now withdraw the offer.'

'But you can't! You're an agent!'

'But not a public one!' Dismissing him, he urged Githa forward and into the hotel.

'Then I'll send it to someone else!'

'Do,' Henry invited cordially under his breath. 'And if that's disapproval I can feel coming off you in waves, Githa, you can eat alone.'

She grinned. 'It isn't. It's approval. I haven't heard such an impressive put-down since—Churchill.'

He glanced at her, raised his eyebrows, and her grin widened.

'I don't like being accosted in the street either,' she said softly. 'I mean, you don't go up to a surgeon and ask him to perform a small operation when he's going for his dinner, do you?'

'Not unless you wish to have a scalpel inserted where you wouldn't want one, no,' he agreed. His expression lightening, he ushered her into the dining room where the waiter courteously seated them.

'It might have been a bestseller,' she teased.

'It might.'

'And if it is you'll grit your teeth and pretend you don't care?'

He looked at her, said softly, 'I *never* grit my teeth.' After ordering wine, with only the merest lift of one eyebrow to ask her approval, he continued, 'Explored the town?'

Her smile turning wry, she murmured in amusement, 'Yes, but not thoroughly.'

'And what did you think of it?' he mocked.

'I think it's delightful. Nice people.'

'Yes, they are.'

'Tell me about it,' she ordered as she accepted her menu.

'Certainly. The town grew up round the castle,

which was built to keep out the Welsh. Wool trade,' he murmured.

'Figures,' she grinned.

'Gloves.'

'Gloves?'

'So I believe. Glove-making was a major industry here in the last century. Maybe still is. Read your menu.'

With a little smile, she did as she was told, then watched him as he read his own, watched other people watch him, and felt really rather proprietorial.

'You're looking smug,' he observed softly.

'Am I?'

'Yes. Why?'

'Because I like being with you. I'll have the salmon.'

He smiled, folded the menus and handed them to the waiter with their order.

When they'd eaten, were slowly savouring their coffee, the woman seated behind Githa started coughing—a harsh, hacking cough that sounded awful. Worried, Githa turned, offered her a glass of water.

'All right?' she asked gently, when the woman had finally got herself under control.

'Oh, yes, dear. I'm ever so much better since I gave up smoking.'

Githa heard Henry choke, and she bit her lip, turned quickly away. Eyes alight with laughter, she stared at him, saw her own thoughts mirrored on his face.

'Unconscious irony,' he murmured as he quickly finished his coffee. 'I love it.' Leaving enough money to cover the bill, he helped her to her feet. Hustling her outside, he caught her hand in his, and gave in to his amusement.

'I wonder what she was like *before* she gave up smoking!'

'I don't know,' she laughed. Leaning her head against his shoulder as they walked slowly back towards the car, she gave a gentle sigh. 'Poor lady.' Looking up, she examined the heavens. 'You can see the stars here.'

'Yes, but you'd do better to look where you're walking.'

She flicked him a grin, continued her contemplation of the sky. 'You can hardly see any stars in London.'

'No.' He courteously held back the branches of a tree that was overhanging a wall so that she could pass through, but unfortunately one slipped free.

'Mind my face,' she cried urgently, and quickly ducked her head. 'Did it scratch me?'

He stared at her, expressionless, eyes almost cold. 'No,' he replied, and walked on.

Staring after him, her own expression thoughtful, she caught him up. 'I have a perfume launch in a few days,' she said quietly, and he halted, turned to look at her. 'They won't be very pleased if I turn up with a scratched face.'

'No,' he agreed slowly. 'Any more than they would if it was sun- or wind-burned. I'm sorry.'

'You thought I was being vain, didn't you?'

'Yes. My mistake. Another one.'

Puzzled, she echoed, 'Another one?'

'Yes.' With a sudden, rueful smile, he touched gentle fingers to her face, and then he stilled, stared at her mouth. 'This is becoming absurd,' he murmured softly. 'Utterly, impossibly absurd.'

'What is?' she whispered, but she knew. This—attraction was getting out of hand.

Staring at him, blocking the narrow pavement, she felt ill again, wanting him.

'You turn me on,' he said, almost to himself. 'Endlessly.' Stepping back, he gave another twisted smile. 'Come on, before we get arrested for loitering with—intent.'

Swallowing hard, she turned her face away. 'Where to?'

'Back to the Hall; I have some reading to catch up on.'

She nodded. And was reading a euphemism for—other things?

It wasn't.

Leaving him in the lounge, feet up on the coffee table, manuscript on his lap—attention not very fixed, she thought—and the dogs curled before the fire, she went into the kitchen to make herself a cup of tea.

Seeing his newspaper on the table, she glanced at the headline, and then slowly sat to read the article—and cried. Although what there was to cry about when a small girl had saved the life of her mother she had no idea. But children, doing whatever, always made her cry. Her throat would block, tears would fill her eyes, and with no encouragement at all, before she knew where she was, she was crying.

She didn't hear Henry come in, just sniffed, searched frantically for a hanky.

'Githa?'

Glancing guiltily round, she sniffed again, quickly averted her face.

Walking across to her, he put a gentle hand on her shoulder, stared into her tear-stained face. 'Ah, don't. He's not worth it.'

With another sniff, she looked up, puzzled. 'What? Have you got a handkerchief?'

He tutted, looked round, walked across to the dresser and snatched up a box of tissues, gave them to her.

Taking one, she blew her nose hard.

Palm warm on her nape, soothing, he repeated, 'He's not worth it, Githa.'

'Who isn't?'

'The man who's stalking you!'

'What? Oh, no, that wasn't why I was crying!'

'Then, why?'

She pointed at the newspaper.

He glanced at the article, glanced at her face.

Embarrassed, she looked away. 'I can't help it,' she mumbled. 'Children just get to me. And she's only four.'

'Yes,' he agreed drily.

'I mean, to phone for an ambulance, get her mother a sugary drink... Diabetes,' she murmured foolishly, then sniffed again. 'I'll make a lousy mother.'

'A wet one, certainly. And if it upsets you so much why on earth are you reading it?'

'Because I'm stupid, I expect. Did you want something?'

'Yes,' he said softly, 'you. But for the moment I'll make do with a cup of coffee. Do you want one?'

She shook her head.

'Then go and explore the house or something. Play with the dogs. But don't go out on your own.'

'Yes, sir, no, sir.'

He gave a wry smile, folded the newspaper over, and went to fill the kettle.

Staring at his averted face, she sighed. Had his gentle concern been a momentary weakness? She could only suppose so. His detachment was back, his preoccupation. And none of this felt real. She wanted him, but she didn't know him. With another sigh, she got to her feet and walked out—before she could touch him, start it up all over again.

Wandering out into the hall, she pushed open a door at random, stared into a rather formal-looking dining room. Closing it, she walked along to the next one, pushed it wide, and wandered in to stare from the French windows at a garden she hadn't known was there. Unlocking the door, she walked out, stared at the dim shapes of rose bushes, shrubs, at the wide lawn that ran the width of the house.

Untying her sweater from round her neck, she put it on properly and continued round towards the back of the Hall. The cool wind sweeping across the valley made her shiver, and she stared up at the sky as she had in Ludlow. There was something really rather comforting about stars. Hundreds and hundreds of them. She could identify the Plough—and very little else, she thought with a wry grin.

Rounding the corner, she pushed through a wrought-iron gate into what looked like a vegetable garden, and then through another gate beside the old stable block—and thought she saw someone up in the trees.

CHAPTER FIVE

SHE didn't stop to think, just reacted. Racing across the cobbled yard, Githa leaped the rockery, ran into the trees—and couldn't see a thing. Used to towns, where even on the darkest night it was still possible to see, here, in the country, it was pitch-dark.

Suddenly frightened, she halted, listened, stared back towards the comforting lights of the Hall. If there was anyone out here, if she was attacked, there would be no one to help. But it seemed so *tame* just to go back. Gritting her teeth, taking a deep breath for courage, she walked cautiously on.

Ears stretched, eyes wide, she listened for the smallest sound—nothing. And then a twig snapped somewhere behind her. Whirling round, eyes narrowed, she grabbed a branch. 'Well, come on, then,' she taunted raggedly. 'Let's see how brave you are face to face!'

'Githa? *Githa!*'

'Henry! There's someone here!' Not waiting, feeling braver now that she knew Henry was nearby, she hurried in the direction she thought the sound had come from, heard one of the dogs bark. Running recklessly on, she suddenly slammed into someone, and screamed with fright.

'What the *hell* do you think you're doing?' Henry demanded savagely.

'For God's sake, Henry, you frightened me to death! I thought...'

'Yes!' he agreed grimly. 'And then what would you have done?'

'You were here...'

'But maybe not near enough! I told you to stay in the Hall.'

'But I saw someone! For goodness' sake, let me go! He'll get away!'

'If there's anyone there, Luther will find him.'

'Yes, but...'

'Don't argue.' With a little shove in the direction of the Hall, he continued furiously, 'You could have been attacked, *murdered*, and I wouldn't have known anything about it!'

'But I saw—'

'And so you ran to investigate. How very clever.'

Halting, grabbing a tree for support on the steep bank, she protested crossly, 'I'm not four! And I am sick to death of always being on the receiving end!'

He didn't answer, just shoved her forward.

Digging in her heels, she pleaded, 'Go and look, Henry. Please just go and look.'

'Not until you're safely in the Hall with the doors locked.'

'But he'll get away!'

'No, he won't. If there is anyone there, Luther will find him.'

'What do you mean, "if"? I heard a twig snap...'

'So? Foxes tread on twigs, badgers—'

'It wasn't a badger. It was a person! Well,' she murmured honestly as she jumped the rockery, 'it was *something*.'

'Or someone,' he completed flatly as he landed beside her. 'Who could have been armed, dangerous, awaiting just such an opportunity!'

'I don't care! Do you have any idea how dirty he makes me feel? To know that he's been watching me when I'm naked! A salacious grin on his face. Leering! I won't put up with it any more! I can't! I've been trying and trying not to let it upset me! But it does upset me! It…'

Reaching out, he pulled her against him. 'I know,' he said quietly.

Resting her head on his shoulder, she shuddered. 'I was scared to death,' she confessed.

'I imagine you were. Come on, into the Hall, and then I'll go and have a look round.'

She changed her mind. Now that the first fright had gone, she didn't want him to go and leave her. 'No, don't go.'

Staring at her in the dim light from the kitchen window, he asked gently, 'Why?'

'Because I'll worry. And supposing he comes to the Hall when you're gone? Maybe I didn't see anyone. Maybe it *was* just a badger. And, if there is someone there, you might get hurt, and… Don't go,' she pleaded.

He stared down at her for some moments in silence, and then they both heard the dog coming back. Panting, tongue lolling, he looked mightily pleased with himself.

'He didn't find anyone,' she stated flatly.

'So it would seem.'

'I'm sorry.'

'So you should be.'

With a lame smile, she asked, 'Did you finish your reading?'

'No.'

'Don't be cross.'

'I'm not.'

'You sound it.'

'Fear has that effect,' he said drily. 'Don't ever do that again.'

Pulling a face, she thought it best to change the subject. 'I have to leave for Paris in a couple of days.'

'I know.'

And then what? she wondered. Would their brief liaison be over? 'Will I see you when I come back?' she asked as casually as she was able.

'Do you want to?'

'Yes,' she said simply.

'Then you will. I'll take you to the airport. Pick you up.'

'Thank you.'

'Stop sulking.'

'I'm not.'

He smiled, a small gleam of mockery in his eyes. 'Come on; you're shivering.' Wrapping a companionable arm round her shoulders, calling the dog with one brief command to come, he urged her towards the back door.

'He doesn't chase sheep?'

'Heaven forbid.'

'That's not an answer.'

And he smiled again, said softly, 'No, Githa, he doesn't chase sheep.' Opening the door, he gently pushed her inside, waited for the dog to pass them, and then locked it.

Taking her hand, he tugged her into the lounge, halted, and stared at her.

'Let's go to bed.'

'It's not bedtime.'

'And when did that ever stop us?' Holding her loosely within the circle of his arms, he murmured, 'I haven't taken in one word of what I've been reading since we came back from Ludlow. I've been growing more and more aroused, more and more fanciful, and I want you naked.'

With that alarming dip in her stomach, that feeling of bones beginning to melt, she stared into his eyes, began to feel hypnotised.

Sliding his fingers into her thick hair, he kissed her. Slowly. Savoured the taste of her, the chill that still lingered on her skin, and her body rested against his, flowed against his. Her arms slid round him, held him. Her eyes closed.

Excitement built slowly, gradually. Breathing became harder, jerkier, and her arms crept up to his back, his shoulderblades, then down in restless little movements that told of her growing agitation, her

growing need. And his mouth continued to ravage
hers with growing urgency, until with a rough,
growled gesture he thrust one hand to her lower spine,
pressed her against him, harder and harder, until fu-
sion seemed likely. Biting into his lower lip, she
tasted blood, and shuddered.

'Not here,' she pleaded raggedly.

'Yes.'

'No.'

He took a deep breath, a steadying breath, lifted his
head. Staring down into her flushed face, his eyes
dark, sleepy, he queried thickly, 'No?'

'No,' she whispered.

'Then go. Quickly.'

For one startled moment, she thought he meant
away from the Hall—meant her to leave—and then
she shuddered, gave a wavering smile. Thrusting herself away, she ran for the door, wrenched it open, and
hared up the stairs to his room.

He reached it first, swept her inside and onto the
massive bed.

Laughing weakly, breathless, she stared at him, felt
her body melt at the way he was watching her.

'Take your clothes off.'

Held by his eyes, she began to do so. He didn't
help. Just watched her.

'Draw the curtains.'

He reached out, switched on the bedside light to
their right, tugged the gold tassel on their left. The
soft drapes slipped free, shielded them from the window. And anyone who might be watching.

'We should have checked the house, the doors, before we...'

'*Before* we?'

And she smiled, remembered the speed with which they'd leaped up the stairs, gave a funny little shrug. 'I left the French doors open...'

'I know. I closed them. And locked them.'

'Good. Why aren't you undressing?'

'Because I'm busy watching you. And because there's something infinitely—arousing about remaining dressed whilst your partner disrobes.'

'Is there?'

'Yes.'

'I'm not sure I like that.'

He held her eyes, trailed one long finger down between her naked breasts. 'You like everything I do to you.'

Yes, except the way he seemed to dismiss her when they weren't making love. As though this was *all* they had. Which she supposed was true. But she didn't want to think about that, because it was somehow shaming. An object of desire. Not a person.

'Get undressed, Henry.'

'In a minute.'

'No, now. Please. Please,' she repeated. 'I don't like feeling so—vulnerable.'

He watched her face for a moment or two longer, and then he nodded, began to undress, and when he was naked he lay beside her, pulled her into his arms. The urgency was gone now, and it was nicer, gentler, more comforting to be made love to in this way. More sharing.

She lay awake for a long time after he'd drifted into sleep, just thinking, wondering if other women ever felt as she felt—a slave to her emotions. Probably. Turning her head on the pillow, she stared at him, wished she could see inside his head. Wished she knew how he really felt about her.

He'd said he was unemotional, but, if he was, *why* was he like that? He'd also said he hadn't expected to like her. Did that mean he *did* like her? Against his own expectations? Needs? Against his will? Perhaps he felt as confused as she did. Then she gave a wry little smile. No, she doubted Henry was ever confused.

Reaching out her arm, she snapped off the bedside lamp and snuggled against his warm body. He grunted, shifted slightly, and eventually, after one or two little jumps when she thought she heard something outside, she too drifted into sleep.

Only to be rudely awakened by the door opening and the overhead light snapping on.

With a little yell of alarm, squinting into the brightness, she sat up in shock as she saw someone outlined in the doorway.

'Oh, my God!' someone exclaimed faintly. 'It's a woman.'

'Then shut the door,' a man answered irascibly.

'But Henry never...'

'Elizabeth! Shut the bloody door!'

Henry moved, stirred, leaned up on one elbow.

'Hello, Mother,' he drawled. 'And Tom's right—do please shut the door.'

It was slammed.

'Mother,' he murmured laconically, and turned over to go back to sleep.

'Henry!' gasped Githa. 'Don't go back to sleep!'

'Why not?'

'Because that was your *mother*!'

'So?'

'So I'm in bed with you! She must have thought…'

'That we were lovers?'

'I've never been so embarrassed in all my life!'

'Then think yourself lucky. If that's all you ever have to be embarrassed about…' He gave a wide yawn, yanked the covers over his bared shoulder and burrowed his head back into the pillow.

'Henry!'

He groaned.

'I'm going home!'

'Don't be ridiculous.'

'It isn't ridiculous. How on earth am I supposed to greet her in the morning?'

'Hello?' he drawled with heavy irony. 'Go to sleep.'

'I can't go to sleep! How can I go to sleep?' she wailed.

He gave a long sigh, rolled over onto his back. 'Githa,' he said with heavy patience, 'I'm thirty-six years old and I imagine my mother knows full well that I'm not a virgin, nor have I been since I was sixteen.'

Diverted, she exclaimed, 'Sixteen?'

'Yes, or thereabouts. Go to sleep.'

He hadn't told her to go to sleep yesterday. Last night he'd made love to her nearly all night long. Which was no doubt why he was tired. As she should have been. With a miffy 'Hmph' she turned over, dragging the covers with her, and determinedly shut her eyes.

He dragged them back, rolled so that his front was against her back, and slid one arm round her to rest on her stomach. She deliberately removed it. 'You said to go to sleep.'

He pressed his mouth to her shoulder.

She twitched it away. And he laughed, rolled her to face him.

'I'm awake now.'

'I don't want you to be awake.'

He smiled. 'So the lady has a temper, does she? That should add spice.'

'I don't want to add spice, and please let go of me.'

His smile widened and his arms snaked round her to hold her close. Very close. 'Don't be a bore, Githa.'

'Why?' she demanded pithily. 'Isn't it allowed?'

'No.'

'Then I'll leave.' Forcing herself away, she sat up, swung her legs out of the bed—and he pulled her back, trapped her beneath his weight. Kissed her until she stopped struggling, stopped trying to fight him off. Kissed her until the magic took over.

'I hate you,' she declared as she lay breathless, satiated.

'Good,' he agreed with a laugh in his voice. 'I hate you too.'

'And I'll never be able to face your mother.'

'Yes, you will; she'll pretend it never happened.'

'Will she?'

'Mmm.' Snuggling her against him, he kissed her shoulder, and went back to sleep.

'Huh.'

In the morning, not only did his mother not pretend it had never happened, she treated Githa with a chilling reserve that would have intimidated an ice cube. And Henry was no help at all.

He introduced her to the tall, regal-looking woman with immaculately styled grey hair, briefly explained why she was there, and then Tom called him, wanting a hand with the suitcases—or to find out what she was doing there. At least, she presumed it was Tom. Henry gave a rueful sigh, directed a long, almost warning look at his mother, and went out.

'I'm sorry…' Githa began.

'Yes,' his mother agreed with lethal politeness, her voice as much like cut glass as her son's. 'But it explains why he told me to go away *now*. Why he offered to come and look after the dogs, doesn't it? I did wonder, of course, because Henry never puts himself out for anyone. Even me. He's as selfish as his father was. Do help yourself to breakfast—I'm sure you know where everything is.' With a look of dislike, she walked out, and Githa just stood there, feeling—diminished.

Hurt, bewildered, angry, she turned on her heel and

went up to Henry's room to pack. He entered just as she was snapping the locks on her suitcase shut.

'What did she say?'

'Nothing.''

'Githa…'

Whirling angrily on him, she demanded, 'Why didn't you warn me of the reception I was likely to get?'

'And what reception did you get?' he asked smoothly. 'What did she say?'

'It wasn't what she *said*, it was the way she said it—as though I were a—a slut! And why?' she cried. 'She doesn't know me! Has never met me before in her life!'

'She knows *about* you,' he said obscurely.

'So? I've never done anything to make her *hate* me!'

'Haven't you?' he queried mildly.

'Haven't I?' she demanded, incensed. 'What does that mean? You know very well I haven't! And what was that long look you gave her? What was that all about?'

'A warning.'

'A warning not to treat me like a slut?'

'No.'

Swinging furiously away, she attempted to tug her case off the bed, and he stopped her, put his hands over hers, removed them from the case.

Turning her to face him, he stared down into her stormy face. 'You're overreacting.'

'No, I'm not. What's going on, Henry? Because

something is, isn't it? Why does your mother dislike me? Or does she automatically dislike any woman you bring here?'

'I don't bring women here. Ever.'

'Then why me?'

There was a little silence, and then he said softly, 'Because I couldn't leave you alone.'

'But wanted to? Wished you could?'

'I don't know,' he admitted quietly. 'Come on, I'll drive you home.'

'You can't drive me home. I have my own car here, and I'm quite capable of driving myself.'

'I didn't say you weren't capable. My mother isn't very good at hiding her feelings,' he explained quietly.

'And what feelings should she have to hide about me? Not going to answer, are you?' she taunted bitterly. 'Why? Because you don't know? Don't care? Or don't want to?'

'Can't. Come on.' Picking up her case, he continued, 'I'll see you down to your car.'

Yes, she thought bitterly. Couldn't wait for her to go, could he? No begging her to stay... Not understanding any of it, hating him, hating herself, she followed him from the room and prayed they wouldn't encounter his mother. They didn't.

Putting her case in the boot, he halted her when she would have climbed behind the wheel. 'Give me five minutes and I'll follow you down.'

'I don't need an escort,' she said angrily. 'I've been driving for *years*!'

'But you haven't had someone stalking you for years. Wait here.'

With an angry toss of her head, she climbed into the car. And waited.

Five minutes later he was back, a bulky envelope tucked under one arm, jacket slung over one shoulder. He threw them into his own car, then walked across to her. Bending down, he waited until she angrily opened the window.

'Don't drive in a temper.'

'Easy to say,' she spat.

'Yes.' With a sigh, he added, 'It's complicated, Githa. I'll explain it to you one day.'

'Thanks!'

'I'll follow you down, then pick you up in the morning to drive you to the airport.'

'I'll get a cab.'

If she expected him to argue, she was mistaken. He gave her a long look, then nodded. 'Very well. I'll see you when you get back.'

'Will you?' she asked moodily.

'Yes.' Ducking his head into the car, he kissed her. She didn't respond, and her look became—colder.

'You don't even *care* do you?'

'Don't I? It's a relationship, Githa,' he added quietly. 'Not a love affair.'

Throwing him an angry look, she fired the engine, waited stiffly for him to withdraw and walk across to his own car, then drove slowly out through the arch. Back to London, to sanity.

He followed her to her door, then drove away, without even a toot of acknowledgement.

She spent a restless night, an angry night, and in the morning, feeling heavy-eyed, she showered, packed and ordered a cab to take her to the airport. It was raining—a depressing drizzle that lowered her spirits even more.

It was also raining in Paris.

Claire, Etienne Varlane's assistant, was there to meet her. She smiled, kissed Githa on both cheeks, and led the way to the car.

'You will not mind going to see Etienne first?' she asked politely. 'Before you book into the hotel? He was most insistent,' she added apologetically.

'No, of course not.' Her mind more on Henry than the powerful boss of Varlane Cosmetics, she stared out at rain-washed streets, at a sea of umbrellas.

And it came as something of a shock when Etienne greeted her with polite reserve, not his usual enthusiasm. Now what?

'Sit down, Githa,' he said, and to his assistant, 'No disturbances, if you please, Claire.'

She nodded, gave Githa a little grimace behind his back, and left.

He sat behind his desk, tossed a package towards her. 'This came a few days ago. Open it.'

A sinking feeling in her stomach, she did so—and discovered why those negatives had been retained. Or at least one of them. The one depicting her naked. So that a print could be sent to Varlane.

'You have seen it before,' he stated.

'Yes,' she agreed tightly as she tore it into shreds.

'Read the note, Githa.'

With a deep sigh, she unfolded the note, stared at it with an expression of distaste. As before, the letters were cut out of a newspaper.

'"If you don't sack her",' Etienne quoted from memory, '"the photograph will be sent to the newspapers. In France and in England".'

'No newspaper would touch it,' Githa protested, without any real hope that it might be true. 'Not something sent anonymously.'

'You think not? I'm not so sanguine. The gutter press will print anything. And sometimes I think that to drag down the famous is their *raison d'être*.'

'I'm not that famous,' she said dully.

'*Non.* But I am.'

'Yes.' She felt sick. Lifting her eyes to his, she asked heavily, 'You're sacking me?'

'No. Not yet. But I am very cross. I gave you the name of a hotel that would be safe for you, staff that could protect you, but you chose not to go there.'

'No,' she whispered. 'A friend lent me her cottage.'

'And this is where the photograph was taken?'

'Yes. There was more than one,' she confessed.

'I see. And so this is the result of your disobedience. We have experience of stalkers, and so we know how to protect our own. But if they will not be guided by us, if they go their own way…

'We've invested a lot of money in you, Githa, and, although I am sympathetic, the business must come first. There is an adverse-publicity clause in your contract, and however unfair it may be—however much none of this may be your fault—if that is published,' he murmured with distaste, 'my business will suffer. We chose you because you look exciting, sophisticated—someone other women can identify with, someone they want to emulate…'

'Yes,' she agreed bitterly. 'Not someone splashed naked across the tabloids.'

'No. And so, reluctantly, we have taken the decision to use another model for the perfume launch tomorrow. We will say that it was always our policy to do so—one girl for the new perfume, our face of the year for the make-up range. You will attend the launch. And you will smile,' he ordered.

'Yes,' she agreed.

'I am sorry.'

'Yes.'

'Find him, Githa. Find him, stop him, or…'

'You will have no alternative but to sack me.'

'*Oui.*' Searching her face, he rang for coffee to be brought in.

'You must have some idea?'

'No,' she denied.

'And the police have been informed of this new development?'

'Yes, Hen—' Breaking off, she bit her lip.

'Hen…?' he prompted.

'Henry,' she sighed. 'A friend of mine.'

'He was with you at the cottage?'

No point in lying. 'Yes,' she agreed.

'So tell me. Tell me about this Henry. About the photographs. The cottage. Tell me all that you know, and perhaps between us we can come up with an idea.'

And so she told him all that had happened—about Henry, the cottage, the graffiti. He already knew about the other incidents.

'And you knew this decorator?'

'No. Henry arranged for him to come.'

'And you trusted him? This man you had only just met?'

'Yes,' she agreed stiffly.

'And now he is your lover?'

'Yes.'

'So soon after meeting?'

'Yes,' she gritted—because Henry had been impossible to withstand. But how could she explain that to Etienne? That there were men in the world who made it impossible to resist. Made sensible thoughts fly out of your head. Made you feel as though you were so special, so—exciting, that the outcome was preordained.

'And so you have been indiscreet,' Etienne reproved.

'No! No one knew I was going to the cottage!' she insisted.

'Except this Henry,' he said softly, 'who is the friend of Cindy, who also worked for the airline. Did she wish to be in their commercial? Did she apply to be our face of the year?'

'No,' she replied helplessly. 'I thought I would be

safe there. And you checked the applicants when the stalker first contacted me!'

'Only the short-list. I will ask Claire to search more diligently. And you also must check.'

'Yes, but I don't think Cindy ever applied. She didn't say…'

'But maybe she did. Maybe she was disappointed. Maybe she told her friend…'

'No!'

'And maybe the friend is—more than a friend.'

'No!'

'But it is possible? *Non?* You know very little about him, and he would know your movements from this Cindy, with whom you are very good friends. You chat to her, tell her what you are doing, where you are going…'

'No,' she denied. But she did. Although she hadn't told her about meeting Henry, had she? Why? she wondered. Why hadn't she told her about him? But it *couldn't* be Henry! He had no *reason*! And for someone to do all that and still make love to her… No.

'Then if not this Henry, it is someone else you know,' Etienne insisted. 'It nearly always is.'

CHAPTER SIX

'Go now to your hotel,' Etienne said, more kindly. 'Think about what I have said. You will attend the launch tomorrow, smile, be friendly, relaxed, and then go home and find out who is doing this to you. And, if I were you, I would find out from the agency that made the airline commercial whether this Cindy wished to be the star.'

Getting to her feet, Githa nodded, walked disconsolately out to the waiting Claire. No point in offering her a discreet hotel now, was there? The damage had been done.

'I'm so sorry,' the French girl said sympathetically. 'Yes.'

'If there is anything I can do…'

'Thank you.'

After booking into the hotel, she went straight up to her room. Not Henry, she insisted to herself. It couldn't be Henry.

But Henry didn't like her. And his mother had been positively venomous. And he would have known her movements, wouldn't he? And he'd been very keen to get the graffiti removed as soon as possible, hadn't he? Because it had been evidence? Or because he cared? Perhaps he'd got fed up with being a stalker

121

from a distance. Perhaps he'd wanted to see her reaction first-hand...

No! Not Henry. Please, God, not Henry.

But supposing it was? Supposing he wrote and told
the newspapers all about their lovemaking? Her response? Sent it in with the photograph...?

Perhaps he'd been taping their conversations...

No! Don't be paranoid, Githa.

But she was about to lose her job, wasn't she?
About to lose a lucrative contract. And if she lost that
she would lose her house, because she wouldn't be
able to afford the bills, would she? Living in
Kensington was expensive. And who else would em-
ploy her after such publicity?

Lying on her bed in the hotel, she went over and
over it—denial, accusation, worry. But if it *was*
Henry...

With an impatient movement, she got to her feet,
collected some of the hotel stationery, and sat at the
desk to make a list of everyone she knew. People
she'd known a long time, people only recently met.
He didn't even have to be English, did he? He, or she,
could be French. You could buy English newspapers
in France, cut out the words, send them...

But the early ones had been posted in England, the
later ones just left in her mail basket. That didn't matter; it could be someone who travelled. But why had
no one ever seen anything? Why had no one ever *seen*
anyone put letters in her basket? Because it *was* someone she knew? Someone the neighbours knew? But
she didn't *want* it to be someone she knew! Couldn't

bear that, she thought. Much better for it to be someone anonymous.

Tossing down her pen, she put her head in her hands, sighed in despair. And even if she did find a suspect how would she ever prove it?

She ate in her room, went to bed early—but not to sleep—and in the morning she stared despondently at her tired face in the mirror. Etienne would *not* be pleased if she attended the launch looking like a wet dish-rag.

She took a cold shower, meticulously made up her face, styled her hair, and went to the perfume launch with a smile pasted to her face. Stared at everyone she met. Wondered.

The press made a great deal of the change in models, but she answered their questions, smiled, posed with the new girl, and escaped as soon as she could.

And on the flight home she stared from the window, and thought. She spent all that night thinking, and the following morning—unsettled, anxious—she wandered from room to room, gave a violent start when the front doorbell pealed. Knew it would be Henry.

Taking a deep breath, she opened the door to him—and even after just a few days' absence his impact was enormous. She wanted to touch him, hold him, and it was a physical *ache* not to be able to. She also knew she'd been lying to herself. She *was* in love with him, and she wasn't sure she could afford the luxury.

Luxury? It wasn't a luxury. It was a feeling of unparalleled need. She wanted nothing more than to hurl herself into his arms, beg for reassurance. But she couldn't do that, could she? Because if it *was* him...

Examining his face, his eyes—eyes that appeared infinitely colder than when they had last met—she silently invited him in.

He wasn't a fool, his perceptions were always razor-sharp, and his eyes narrowed on her tired face.

'What's wrong?'

'Nothing,' she denied, and wondered at her duplicity. But she was tired, and hurting, and worried, and so it seemed best not to tell anyone anything. Even Henry.

Leading the way along the tiny hall and into the bright kitchen, she turned, tried to view him objectively, see him through fresh eyes, tried to ignore the attraction, the magnetism that flowed between them. The tension.

'Still sulking?'

She shook her head, barely even registered what he'd said, or the coldness in his voice, because her mind was filled with Etienne's words.

'No kiss?' He sounded mocking, derisive.

Was it him? And did he think she knew?

Worriedly staring at him, she blurted, 'Henry...' And then didn't know how to continue. Turning away, she fiddled aimlessly with a pot plant on the window sill. 'It *isn't* you, is it?' she pleaded.

'Isn't me, what?'

'Only Etienne said...'

'Etienne?'

'Varlane, head of the cosmetic company. He

said…' Swivelling back, she stared at his closed face, despaired. But she had to ask. 'To come here when the graffiti had just been sprayed on my wall, to say you wanted me when you didn't know me…' she murmured distressfully. 'And you and Cindy were the only ones who knew I was going to Shropshire.'

Searching his grey eyes, eyes that were cold and distant, she swallowed hard. 'And you weren't in any of the photographs…

'And it was you who told the police,' she suddenly remembered. 'But they didn't come and ask to see the photographs, did they? You *wouldn't* do that to me, Henry, would you?'

He stared at her, just watched her, and then he asked quietly, flatly, 'You are accusing me of being the man who is stalking you? Frightening you?'

'Not *accusing*!' she denied in anguish. 'But I've been thinking and thinking, and—'

'Goodbye, Githa.' Turning, he walked away.

'Henry!'

The front door was closed with a snap of finality.

Face twisted, wretched, she picked up the pot plant and threw it at the wall. Lip quivering, she slumped at the table, slapped the surface hard, then sprang to her feet, ranged aimlessly round the small kitchen.

'I love you!' she shouted. 'But I have to *know*!'

And he hadn't denied it, had he? Hadn't tried to calm her, soothe her. In fact, he'd looked at her as though he'd *expected* her not to like him any more. Why?

Hurt, bewildered, frightened, she kicked irritably at a chair-leg that got in her way.

If it *was* him, there had to be a reason. And the only reason there could possibly be was Cindy. Perhaps that was why his mother had been so scathing. Perhaps he and Cindy *were* closer than friends. And, if they were, and his mother had found Githa with her son…

But he *couldn't* have made love to her if he'd been in love with someone else! And it couldn't be Cindy. Cindy was her friend! Cindy would have *told* her if she and Henry were close. Wouldn't she? Would have told her if she was angry about something.

But perhaps she wasn't. And perhaps there were men who could make love to one woman whilst being in love with another… Eyes thoughtful, frowning, she stared at the wall. He'd said, hadn't he, that he'd misinterpreted Cindy's words about her…?

But supposing he thought he *hadn't* misinterpreted them? Supposing he believed she'd spent her life putting Cindy down? And if he thought that Cindy should have been Miss Varlane… 'Cheating bitch'… That could fit, couldn't it?

Never, ever had she yearned so much to have someone to talk to. A sister, a mother. Someone who would understand. Really understand. But she didn't have anyone, and she needed to find out if Cindy had wanted to be Miss Varlane. Had wanted to be in the airline commercial. Because if she had…

Snatching up the phone, rifling impatiently through her directory, she found the number of the agency that had handled the airline commercial. Asked to speak to Lisa, who had handled the account.

'I know it's probably not ethical, and not allowed, or something, but I need to know who applied to be in the commercial for the airline. Who was short-listed. What? Oh, sorry,' she apologised lamely. 'It's Githa James. Please, Lisa, it's really important.'

Lisa told her. Two names had been short-listed— Alison Dear and Mandy Crowe. Neither of which was Cindy. And neither of which she knew.

Relieved, thankful, but no further enlightened, she slowly replaced the receiver. If not Cindy, then it couldn't be Henry, could it? So now what? How did you find a stranger?

But Henry hadn't been in the photographs, hadn't ever been with her when one was taken...

Worry and despair hovering like a cloud above her, she walked heavily upstairs, took out all the notes that had been sent over the past three months. She reread them, examined them for clues, any reference—however nebulous—to the airline. To Varlane. But they weren't specific. None of them was specific. Just distressing. Malicious. And it couldn't be Henry. Nor Cindy. So who was left?

Perhaps Cindy knew of someone, had heard gossip at the airline...

But then, surely, if she had, she would have told her. Cindy was her friend. Cindy had been pleased when she'd been asked to do the commercial. Had told her to accept. She hadn't said she was putting anyone's nose out of joint.

Which left what? Someone unknown. Unless it was Alison Dear or Mandy Crowe. But she didn't even *know* them! Didn't think she'd ever spoken to either of them in her life! And if she didn't find out soon she would lose her job. Had perhaps already lost Henry…

Shoving the letters back in the drawer, she slammed it shut, sat with her head in her hands, tried to think.

She had some lunch, cleaned the house, but her mind wouldn't *stop*. It churned uselessly, pointlessly, and then the phone rang and she went to stand by it, waited for the intercepting device to kick in, then snatched it up when she recognised Cindy's voice.

'Hi.'

Trying to inject a note of enthusiasm into her voice, she forced a smile. 'Hello, Cindy, how are you?'

'Me? I'm fine. How was the cottage? Enjoy yourself? How was Paris?'

With a bitter little smile, Githa murmured listlessly, 'Paris was fine. And the cottage—thank you for lending it to me. Cindy—did you tell anyone I was there?'

'Tell anyone? No, why?'

'Oh, no reason.'

'There must be a reason!' Cindy laughed. 'And you sound awfully depressed.'

'Do I? Just tired, I expect.'

'Nothing to do with Varlane?'

'Varlane?'

'Mmm. Just wondered if they were being picky about your stalker. They do *know* about him?'

'Yes.'

'Oh, good. And they haven't *sacked* you or anything?'

'Sacked me? Why would they sack me?'

'Oh, I don't know. I was just worrying about you, was all.'

'Oh, thanks. Cindy?'

'Yes?'

About to ask her about the airline commercial—whether she'd ever heard anything—Githa changed her mind. 'It doesn't matter; nothing important.'

They chatted for a few minutes more, and neither of them mentioned Henry. Perhaps Henry hadn't told Cindy about their—liaison. So why hadn't *she*? Because her affair with Henry was none of Cindy's business—and because it couldn't be Cindy who was disrupting her life. *Couldn't*.

But it was still best not to tell anyone anything.

The next morning a fluffy toy cat was left on her doorstep. Its face had been viciously disfigured. Feeling sick again, ill, Githa quickly disposed of it.

And the day after that there was a brown envelope containing a page torn from a newspaper—and there she was. Naked. The caption splashed across her knees declared, THE VARLANE GIRL AS YOU'VE NEVER SEEN HER! She didn't bother to read what else it said. Crumpling it, she tore it into tiny pieces. She asked the neighbours if they'd seen anything, anyone, and they all shook their heads. So that was that. There didn't seem much point in telling the police.

Half an hour later, Etienne Varlane rang. Personally. He'd just received a similar package.

'I'm sorry, Githa.'

'Yes,' she agreed listlessly.

'If any of the other newspapers ring I will make it clear that you are being victimised, that the picture was taken without your knowledge, your consent. But...'

'Yes,' she agreed. 'But.'

'I am sending you a severance cheque...'

'Thank you. That's generous.'

'I *am* generous. And very, very sorry. We will miss you. You have been a great pleasure to work with. I am also sending you a list of the names of the models who applied to be face of the year.'

'Thank you.'

'Lucinda Barton's name is on it. Good luck, Githa,' he concluded quietly, and the receiver was replaced.

Replacing her own, she automatically wiped away the tears, bit her lip hard. Lucinda's name was on it? she thought hazily. She'd never said she'd applied. Perhaps she'd forgotten. Perhaps she hadn't thought it very important. Or perhaps she'd told Henry. Because everything always seemed to come back to Henry, didn't it? 'The man's dangerous,' the studio assistant had said. Trampled on people's sensibilities. Their aspirations.

Taking a shallow breath, trying to ease the tight, painful ache in her chest—the feeling that her lungs weren't going to work properly—she wanted to run away, hide, be anywhere but where she was, be anyone but who she was. How many people had seen the newspaper? she wondered. How many people who knew her? Knew she was the Varlane girl? Had been, she corrected with a bitter twist to her mouth. Had been.

And the note sent to Etienne had said to sack her.

Two days ago Cindy had asked if she'd been sacked.

No, she'd said.

And Cindy was on the list.

Coincidence?

She should have asked Etienne if anyone had rung to ask if she'd been sacked.

But it couldn't be Cindy.

And so it had to be Henry. *Had* to be. She hadn't believed it, because she hadn't wanted to believe. And Henry's mother had been—hateful. Because Cindy was like a daughter to her? Because she knew that her son loved her?

She had to go and see Cindy, hadn't she? Ask her about Henry. Not even bothering to comb her hair, she snatched up her bag and her car keys, shoved her feet into flat shoes, and went to find her. It was a place to start. A process of elimination. She should have asked her about Henry when he'd first appeared.

Cindy wasn't at her flat. Her neighbour said she'd gone up to Shropshire for the weekend. Which, presumably, meant the cottage. Or the Hall. So Githa drove to Shropshire. She'd had no breakfast, and now no lunch, she was tired, aching—and she needed to know.

Cindy wasn't at the cottage. So she had to be at the Hall. Githa stopped briefly to ask the farmer if he'd seen her, and he laughed. 'Seen her? I do nothing else *but* see her! Last week, this weekend, but, yes—' he smiled '—I saw her earlier going up towards the Hall. You surely do live in each other's pockets, you two. Nice to have friends.'

'Yes,' she agreed weakly, and in a great deal of puzzlement. Last week? This weekend? But Cindy hadn't been up here last week... Unless Cindy and Henry were in it together.

With that sick feeling inside, not wanting a confrontation—confirmation—but knowing she must have it, she drove to the Hall. Ringing the front doorbell, she waited, stared sightlessly over the valley. Shut her mind to everything. Ask first, she cautioned herself. There was probably a very simple explanation. Cindy had probably come up to see if she was getting on all right in the cottage, hadn't been able to find her, and so—what? Left again?

It was Cindy who answered the door—and Githa knew. Finally, she knew. Knew by the shocked look in Cindy's baby-blue eyes, by her automatic reaction to shut the door. She made a swift recovery, smiled, but it was too late.

Just Cindy? Or Cindy and Henry?

'Why?' Githa asked quietly.

'Why what?' she laughed. 'And don't stand out there—come in.'

'No, thank you,' Githa replied with awful politeness. 'Just tell me why. Don't deny it. Don't tell me you didn't do it, didn't mean to do it. Just tell me why.'

'Githa, I don't know what you're talking about!'

'Yes, you do.'

And it was as if a shutter came down. Gone was the Cindy she had known from the age of eleven; gone was the gentle, humorous expression. Her blue eyes became hard, her mouth a grim line. 'Why?' she asked coldly. 'I'll tell you why. Because you always take what I want.'

'Don't be absurd.'

And Cindy gave a mirthless smile. 'Yes. Your answer to everything—"don't be absurd",' she mimicked. 'If it doesn't fit in with your notions, it's absurd. Isn't it? Absurd for me to want to be in the airline commercial, absurd for me to want to be face of the year...'

'But you didn't *want* the airline commercial! You said you didn't!'

'Of course I did! What else was I supposed to say? And I've had a lot of practice at smiling in the face of adversity, haven't I?'

'What's that supposed to mean?'

'That you take it all. You always did.'

'But we were friends!'

'Were we? Do you know why I never invited you back to my home?'

Bewildered, she shook her head.

'You never even *wondered*?'

'No,' Githa replied. And Cindy laughed. A scornful, scoffing laugh.

'No,' she agreed, 'because you never wonder about anything, do you? Just take it all for granted. Well, I never asked you, *Githa*, because I couldn't have borne to have your name thrown in my teeth every five minutes. How wonderful you were, how nice.'

'Don't be abs…'

'Absurd?' she mocked. 'But it isn't. People do it all the time. You must be the most *liked* person in the universe! At school, at work…'

'Then why on earth did you remain my *friend*?' Githa demanded in perplexity. 'If you disliked me so much, why *remain* friends with me?'

'Because coming second was better than not coming anywhere at all. As your "friend" I was someone. You were always the winner—took everything, didn't you? Without effort, without even trying. Always in the thick of everything, the leader of everything—sports, lessons, mischief—and so, by association, was I. Without you, no one would have noticed me. I like to be noticed. So I became your friend. And I would have remained your friend—if you hadn't taken the part I so desperately wanted.'

'The airline commercial,' Githa stated.

'Yes.'

'But if it hadn't been me…'

'It would have been someone else? Oh, yes, I know that. I just didn't want it to be you. And you said you didn't want it.'

'I didn't.'

'But you got the part, didn't you? By sucking up to the producer, the director…'

'I've never sucked up to anyone in my life!'

'Haven't you? Then how come you get the prizes? Always laughing, always smiling; everyone likes you, don't they? "Oh, that Githa's a nice girl",' she mimicked. '"Do anything for anyone. Isn't Cindy lucky to have such a kind friend? Aren't you lucky, Cindy?" But I was prettier, cleverer, so how come I didn't get the plums? How come you got the commercial? How come you got to work for Varlane?'

'Because I was photogenic,' Githa murmured foolishly. She found she couldn't even be angry. Just— helpless. Distraught. 'And so you set out to punish me?'

'Yes. And that's where it would have stayed—an irritation, a nuisance—but you had to go one step further. You had to have Henry too.'

Not Henry. Thank God, not Henry.

'And that wasn't allowed?' she managed sadly.

'No. I watched you,' she said with utter distaste. 'Both of you. And it was disgusting. On the kitchen *floor*!'

Oh, dear God.

'Henry doesn't *behave* like that! He's fastidious and elegant! He would *never* behave in such a disgusting fashion! But you had to have him, didn't you? Had to seduce him! Make him look stupid…'

'No…'

'Yes!' she hissed. 'I managed to keep you apart for years, because I *knew* what would happen, knew he'd be taken in by your smarmy ways. And then he saw that commercial—' Breaking off, she took a deep breath, continued even more bitterly, if that was possible. 'Tried to keep it secret, didn't you? *He* didn't tell me. *You* didn't.'

Still following her own train of thought, Githa murmured, 'And so you lent me the cottage because it would make it easier to stalk me. But you didn't expect that Henry would come too, didn't know that we'd met, did you?' And she knew from Cindy's tight expression that she was right. 'And so you followed me…'

'I've been following you everywhere,' she agreed, almost smugly.

'But how?' Githa demanded in bewilderment. 'You were at work! I dropped you off!'

'And I walked inside, but when you were gone I walked out again, rang in sick from a public booth. I collected my car from the car park…'

'All planned,' she whispered sadly.

'Of course. I knew you would offer me a lift to the airport.'

'And then you saw me with Henry—and took the photographs.'

'Yes. Good, weren't they?'

'No, Cindy, they were sick. As you are obviously sick. And a coward. You judge others by yourself, give them motives only you have, and that's really rather foolish. All you had to do was say that you desperately wanted to be in the commercial and I would have stood down. All of this could have been avoided.'

'Could it?' Cindy asked with a disbelieving sneer. 'I don't think so.'

'No,' Githa agreed tiredly, 'perhaps not. You enjoyed it, didn't you?'

'Yes. And stupid, forgiving little Githa won't even prosecute, will she?'

'No,' she agreed, 'stupid, forgiving little Githa won't even prosecute.' Feeling heart-sick, shattered, she stared at Cindy's face—a face she thought she had known so well—and watched it change again. She hadn't heard a car, hadn't heard anything but Cindy's bitter words, and so she was surprised when Cindy's face suddenly crumpled and she ran past Githa—and into Henry's arms.

Turning, Githa stared at them. Henry stared back, held his friend in a warm embrace as she sobbed out accusations she said Githa had hurled at her.

Githa had never seen him in a suit. Or a raincoat. And he looked distant, unfamiliar. But so very, very elegant. And when Cindy had lapsed into silence, he said coldly, 'I was on my way to the airport and I passed a news stand. ''Varlane girl as you've never seen her'', the billboard said. And so I stopped, bought a newspaper that I've never bought in my life. Concerned about you, worried about you, I turned the car around, came to find you. I went to Cindy's flat in case you were there. A neighbour said Cindy had come up here, and that you had been looking for her.'

'And so here you are,' she said dully.

'Yes, and so here I am,' he agreed, in a voice that would have chipped varnish, an upper-class drawl that was so effectively decimating. 'You accused me, and now you've accused Cindy. Want to go for the triple? What about my mother? Tom? It could be a family conspiracy.'

'But isn't. And now there's no longer any concern or worry, is there?'

'No. Goodbye, Githa. Don't come back, will you?'

'No,' she agreed sadly, 'I won't come back.' Searching his face, a face that was so very familiar, she added even more sadly, 'I loved you. Did you know that? I finally fell in love with you.'

'Did you?' he asked without interest.

'Yes.' With a broken little smile, she walked to her car on legs that felt rubbery and drove away. She didn't think she had ever hurt so much in her entire life. To be hated, and not know you were hated, for sixteen years. Really hated... To like someone, to think you were liked in return... Best friends...

And to finally fall in love, and then have it thrown back in your face.

She didn't know where she drove, didn't know which turnings she took, didn't look at signposts, just inwards. Went over and over and over it. How could she not have known? Guessed? How could a friend-ship that had lasted most of her life have been based on a lie?

She didn't think about her own situation at all. Didn't think about losing her job, the possibility of losing her house, or the fact that her agent would be frantically trying to get in touch with her if she'd seen the newspaper or heard from Varlane. She just thought about Cindy, about what she had done out of jealousy and spite. So much *bitterness*.

She thought about Henry. Had he known? Suspected that it might be Cindy?

Why should he? *She* hadn't.

And how could she have been so blind? Had she really just swanned through her life without thinking about anyone else at all? Not considered anyone's feelings? She had thought herself lucky, had assumed her friends would be pleased for her, as she would have been pleased if the positions had been reversed. She'd never been jealous, envious—had she just sailed through life with a sublime disregard for anyone else? What other emotions had she generated in people's breasts that she had no knowledge of?

Yet she hadn't set out to be in the airline commercial. Hadn't *wanted* to be in it. Varlane had contacted her, not the other way about. And at school? What had she done at school to make her hated? She'd been good at sports, reasonably good academically—and head girl. Yes, she'd been head girl. Was that a role Cindy had wanted too? But she'd been *voted* head girl, and she'd found it embarrassing.

Someone hooted, flashed their lights at her, and she blinked, realised it was getting dark. Quickly putting on her lights, she stared round her in bewilderment. Nothing seemed familiar, and she hadn't the faintest idea where she was—wasn't sure she cared.

She twice stopped for petrol, only because the warning buzzer on the dashboard told her she was dangerously low. Without that she'd probably have run out, been stranded somewhere. And she hurt. Hurt so much. Couldn't leave it alone. Kept thinking over and over it. Would the gutter press come knocking on her door, wanting an exclusive? She'd go away, she thought. Make a clean break, a fresh start. She had enough money for her immediate needs; a cheque from Varlane was on its way. Etienne Varlane had said he'd been generous...

In fact, she didn't need to go home at all, did she? Not for a while. The bank paid her bills... Jenny had a key, could keep an eye on the place, collect her post...

The more she thought about it, the more attractive it seemed. A month, she decided. She'd tour round for a month, see all the places she had never seen— York, the borders. Due to her inattention, she was halfway there already. She'd stop at the next hotel she came to... She could always buy some clothes, toiletries...

One month later, the first day of June, she finally returned to Kensington, and stared at her little mews house as though it were unfamiliar, as though she'd never seen it before in her life. She could sell it, she thought, move away. She might need to, she thought with a bitter smile, because there was the distinct possibility that she was pregnant. She might not be, of course, might be late because of all the upsets, the worry. But she'd forgotten to take the pill once or twice at the cottage. She'd taken them *late* when she'd remembered, but...

That would be the final irony, wouldn't it? To be having the child of a man who didn't like children, didn't want a wife, a family. And, even if he did, he no longer liked her, did he? And so, if she was pregnant, she would have to move. Henry's office was just round the corner from her house, and she couldn't risk the possibility of bumping into him from time to time, could she? Risk the possibility of him seeing her grow fatter and fatter...

With a sad, weary little sigh, she put her head on the steering wheel, wondered if life could actually get any worse. For the last few weeks she'd been burying her head in the sand, changing hotels each night, driving, moving on, and she remembered none of it.

Climbing tiredly from the car, she collected her new luggage and let herself into the house. It didn't feel like home any more.

Half an hour later, someone rang her bell. Assuming it was Jenny with her post, she opened the door—and found Henry there.

CHAPTER SEVEN

HE WAS still wearing his raincoat and had his back towards her, brown silky hair curling across the collar, and she wanted to weep.

He slowly turned, stared at her tired face, said quietly, 'Hello, Githa.' His eyes were no longer cold. Just rather sad.

Wrenching her gaze away, she stared bleakly at nothing. 'Go away, Henry.'

'No.' Stepping inside, he closed the door behind him, and she hastily retreated to the kitchen. He followed.

'How have you been? Stupid question; I can see how you've been.'

'Yes.'

'*Where* have you been?'

'Away,' she said dismissively.

'Away where?'

'Somewhere, nowhere. Does it matter?'

'No,' he agreed, sounding as tired as she. 'I left the Hall not five minutes after you, drove like a maniac, got here by seven, and then sat in my car until the following morning. Just waiting. I didn't know whether you'd had an accident, broken down... Didn't know whether to call the police. If it hadn't been for Jenny telling me you'd rung...' Impatiently shoving

142

back a lock of hair that had fallen over his forehead, he stared at her, caught her shoulders, pulled her gently towards him.

Flinching away, she gritted, 'Don't.'

'No,' he agreed. 'Hardly appropriate, is it? In the circumstances.'

'How did you know I was back?'

He gave a grim smile. 'There was a message on my answer machine when I got back from the States just now. I'd paid someone to watch the house, let me know when they saw your car.'

'I see. And what is it that you want?'

'To talk to you, explain... I had to go to New York. I'd already changed the flight more times than... I couldn't *keep* postponing the damned meeting!'

'No.' Retreating behind the table, she watched him. Waited. As he had once watched her.

'I saw her face,' he added quietly. 'After you'd gone. Just for a fleeting moment, in my wing mirror. She was smiling—not hurt, upset. Smiling. Like a satisfied little cat. And I knew.'

'You knew before,' she argued.

'I'm sorry?'

'You knew before,' she repeated. 'Knew something, anyway, when you came after I got back from Paris. You were—different.'

He didn't even need to think back, he just stared at her, slowly nodded. 'Not about Lucinda—not that.'

'Then, what?' she asked without interest.

'About Matthew,' he said quietly. 'Your one and only lover.'

'Matthew?' she queried in bewilderment. 'What about Matthew?'

'That you still saw him, that his marriage had broken up, that you were...'

'What?' she demanded. 'That we were what?'

'Still lovers.'

'Still *lovers*? Are you mad?'

'Probably,' he agreed tiredly. 'You didn't tell me Lucinda knew him.'

'Of course she knew him! She knew all my friends! Why wouldn't she? We were *close*! We made up foursomes! Me and Matthew, she and whatever current boyfriend she had!'

'Yes,' he agreed on a sigh. 'He's a photographer, isn't he?'

'Yes. So?'

He waited, watched her, slowly saw the realisation dawn on her face. 'No,' she denied hoarsely. 'I *won't* believe that Matthew had anything to do with Cindy's plan to hurt me!'

'No! No, I only meant that he showed her how to use his developing equipment. He didn't know what she wanted it for. I was only trying to...' Thrusting his hands through his hair, he began again. 'Lucinda knew Matthew. She happened to mention him the day you were due back from Paris. She didn't know that I knew about him... I didn't *think* she knew that I knew about him because I didn't *think* she knew about us! But she said you were lovers. *Still* lovers! That it had broken up his marriage. And so, when I came to see you, I was angry.'

'But you couldn't ask, could you?' she derided bitterly. 'Just walked out when I asked you—'

'Accused...'

'*Asked!* Go away, Henry,' she ordered flatly. 'I don't think we have anything left to say to each other.' Turning her back, she stared from the window. Except that she might be pregnant. But she couldn't tell him that, could she?

'Githa...'

'*Go away!*' she shouted.

He sighed.

'And don't sigh at me. You have absolutely *no* idea what I've been going through...'

'Yes, I do,' he argued wearily. 'About on a par with what I've been going through.'

Whirling back to face him, she hissed, '*You* weren't stalked by your best friend. *You* didn't have salacious photographs published. And you weren't sacked!' And you aren't in love.

'No. And I should have guessed what she was up to a long time ago.' Propping his hands on the back of the chair opposite her and leaning his weight on them, he said quietly, 'I should have trusted my own instincts about you, not listened to Lucinda. And the vendetta against you wasn't because of the airline, Githa,' he stated wearily, 'or because of Varlane. It was because of me.'

'Don't be abs—' Breaking off, she bit her lip.

'The vendetta against you was because of me,' he repeated. Eyes sombre, with a rather twisted smile, he continued, 'I thought myself such an excellent judge of character, of human nature. I thought I could look at someone and know what they were like. I've known Lucinda since she was five years old—and I never knew how she felt. She did it for me,' he added bitterly. 'She was hysterical, pleading; she said she did it for me,' he concluded in distaste.

'Something else I took,' she murmured.

'Sorry?'

'Nothing.' With a deep, ragged sigh, she searched his face. He looked as tired as she felt. 'The photographs were because of you, perhaps, but the rest was because of the airline commercial, Varlane.'

'No.'

'Henry! It started when I joined Varlane! I didn't *know* you then.'

'No,' he agreed, 'but I'd shown an interest. Three or four months ago now, I saw you on the television commercial, asked Lucinda about you. Asked if she knew you. "Why?" she said, "Want to meet her?" And I said yes. I didn't notice any bitterness in her voice, any anger. She was just Lucinda. Someone I'd known a long time—familiar, not seen, not noticed. Just Lucinda. People come and go, accepted or not, as the case may be, but I don't *think* about them. I'm cold, unemotional. I don't like people very much.'

'No,' she agreed helplessly.

'I asked her what you were like. Where you lived. She said she didn't know, that you'd just moved.'

'Of course she knew where I lived!'

'Yes. You aren't listed in the phone book…'

'I *know* I'm not listed in the phone book! And she

said she hated me! Had always hated me! At school...'

'No.'

'What do you mean, ''no''? I was there, Henry! I heard her say it!'

With a tired sigh, he explained, 'I meant that at school, work, it was only jealousy, not hatred. The hatred came when I first showed an interest in you. About the same time as you landed the Varlane contract.'

Staring at him, slowly remembering Cindy's words, she argued, 'It only became malicious when I seduced you...'

'Yes. Except you didn't.'

'No. But perfect Henry could never be a seducer, could he?'

'No,' he agreed heavily. 'But the letters, the paint, the—annoyances were because of me. She said so.'

'And so it would never have happened if...?'

'No.'

Closing her eyes, feeling sick and shaken, needing to *think* about it, she gave a slight start when he continued quietly.

'Ever since I first saw you, it seems as though I haven't had a moment's peace. It seems for ever since I've had a decent night's sleep. But had I known what I was setting in motion... Dear God, Githa, to put you through all that because of me...'

'Yes.'

'And that day you accused me...'

'I didn't accuse you,' she denied flatly, 'I *asked*

you. And all you had to say was no. I was frightened, upset, hurt. I needed reassurance. If it was you—and it could have been—who could I ask for help? I have no family. I didn't know you, Henry. You weren't in the photographs, you erupted into my life so suddenly... And it was all I could think of—please don't let it be Henry.'

'I was angry,' he said again. 'And, yes, it was a logical enough conclusion for you to make. But I found it hard to reconcile the you I was coming to know with the you Lucinda always intimated you were. The you who was supposedly still having an affair with Matthew.'

'Supposedly?' she scoffed. 'You've just finished telling me that I *was*!'

'That Lucinda said you were—not knowing I knew you, knew about Matthew. She said she was concerned—dammit, she *looked* concerned—said you were storing up heartbreak for yourself! I didn't *know* she knew about us!'

In sharp contrast to his angry tones, she asked quietly, reasonably, 'Why didn't you ever tell her? Because you knew what would happen?'

'No, of course not,' he denied dismissively. 'Because I never tell anyone anything. The photographs of you leaving the Hall that first day were taken from the house. From my bedroom. Which I suspected from the angle, but could not be sure.'

'So she was there in the house when...?' And if they'd made love, as he'd intended that first day...

'Yes. Why didn't *you* tell her, Githa?' he asked

curiously. 'She was your friend—friends gossip, don't they?'

She gave a bitter smile. 'Yes, they gossip, but I didn't want to gossip about that. At first because I was ashamed of the fact that I'd been intimate with a man I barely knew. And later because it had become precious to me. Not something to be gossiped over, shared. And as for Matthew I haven't seen him since he met Christine, his wife. We could have remained friends. We parted amicably. But it wouldn't have been fair on his wife. I didn't know his marriage was in trouble, but Cindy obviously kept in touch with him…'

Eyes wide, suddenly horrified, she whispered, 'If Cindy told Christine that I was having an affair with her husband, and she left him because of it…'

'I don't know,' he replied helplessly. 'But she surely wouldn't wreck a marriage just to get back at me, punish you. All I know is what she said—and that she used his developing equipment for the photographs. I'll find out,' he promised. 'Set it straight if I can. But surely the woman would believe her own husband's denials over Lucinda's accusations?'

'Would she? Why? *You* believed her!'

'Part of me believed her,' he qualified. 'Because models and actresses are *supposed* to be like that. And on film you *do* look like that—slightly wicked, teasing, a hint of exciting possibilities.'

'But I'm *not* like that! It's *acting*, Henry! Miss Varlane wasn't *me*, she was someone else, someone separate…'

'I know now, but I didn't *then*, not at the beginning. I only knew that I wanted you, was attracted to you, and Lucinda was always so plausible. I don't know how she did it, but the more praise she heaped on someone, the more you disliked them. It wasn't a question of damning with faint praise, but decimating with adulation. It was nothing she said, nor the way she said it—and if anyone protested, intimated that she was a lousy judge of character, she would vehemently deny it—but *always* you were left with the impression that the person wasn't very nice.'

'And that included me.'

'It *especially* included you. We all thought you were a scheming opportunist who was using Lucinda for your own ends.'

'But you wanted me,' she said bitterly.

'Yes.' With a hollow smile, he added, 'I've never felt like that. Never behaved like that, but, yes, I wanted you. It was all I could think about. All I could feel. But you weren't someone I could like. You followed Cindy into the airline...'

'*She* followed me,' she corrected as she stared fixedly at the table.

'Tell me.'

She shrugged. 'I joined first, and a few days later she turned up in the induction class. Laughing. And I was pleased to see her,' she added heavily. 'Thought it would be fun to be together.'

Glancing up at him, she gave a bitter little smile. 'And that's why your mother hated me, isn't it? Because she thought I wasn't a nice friend for Cindy to have. Cindy, who was like a daughter to her. And she certainly didn't want her son sleeping with the enemy!'

'Not hated,' he protested. 'But we all thought you were blighting her life. Every class she joined at school, you joined—or so she said. Music, art, games. You followed her into the airline, always managed to get the best long-haul flights, snaffled the airline pilot she was in love with from under her nose...'

'I beg your pardon?' she demanded coldly.

'I don't remember his name, but she saw him coming out of your room somewhere, and—'

'If he was coming out of my room,' she clarified icily, 'then I wasn't in it.'

'I wasn't accusing you, Githa, I was merely telling you what she implied, telling you why we—mistrusted you. And then, when—as we thought—you robbed her of the chance of being in the airline commercial, it seemed the last straw. And she did it so *well*! She'd get over it, she was so happy for you, you deserved it, and we...'

'Thought I was a scheming little bitch who walked over everyone to get what she wanted,' she completed for him.

'Yes.'

'But you still wanted me,' she stated disgustedly. 'Poor you.'

'Yes,' he agreed with bitter irony. 'Poor me. And if it had been any other girl but you that I'd shown an interest in...'

'It wouldn't have happened, would it? But it *was* me—the one who always got what she wanted.'

'Yes. But you had no idea that she desperately wanted to be the stewardess in the commercial, did you?'

'No. She seemed so pleased for me, so delighted.' With a despairing laugh, she exclaimed, 'I must be a lousy judge of character! It never once crossed my mind that she didn't even like me. I thought we were friends. Best friends. I thought she felt about me as I felt about her.'

'You didn't tell the police who it was,' he said quietly.

'No.'

'Why?'

'Because she was my *friend*,' she burst out. 'Because it *hurts*!' Turning away, she walked across to pick up the kettle from the hob, carried it over to the sink.

'Yet she ruined your career, frightened you, hurt you...'

'Yes,' she whispered as she filled the kettle and set it back on the hob. 'Sixteen years. For sixteen years, ever since we were eleven, she was living a lie.'

'No,' he corrected her gently. 'They were grievances that only matured when you...'

'Seduced the man she wanted.'

'And I didn't even know the half of it, did I? Not about the paint she poured over your car—'

'I had it resprayed,' she interrupted flatly.

'About the vacuum-cleaner salesman who attacked

you, wouldn't go away until you were forced to call the police. About the packages and letters sent to Varlane. Why didn't you tell me?'

'I didn't think it would interest you. You seemed to find the whole thing a bore. Told me to pull myself together.'

'No.'

'Yes.' Turning, she stared at him. 'When I got the photographs, you didn't even seem bothered. You weren't angry, upset…'

'Yes, Githa, I was. If I'd found him— What I thought was a him,' he corrected with a grim smile, 'I would have broken both his arms. I asked John to keep a lookout for strangers, informed the local po-lice…'

'Only of course it wasn't a stranger. And no one would have thought twice about seeing Cindy, would they?'

'No. And the dogs would not have barked.'

'And the neighbours never saw anything because Cindy wasn't a stranger. She was my friend. Who was helping me.'

'Yes. She gave me the negatives,' he added. 'I de-stroyed them.'

'*Gave* them to you?'

'Under duress,' he agreed.

She didn't answer, merely turned back to light the gas under the kettle, but she could imagine the duress.

'And when you came back from Paris why didn't you tell me you were about to get the sack? That you'd been replaced for the perfume ad?'

'You didn't give me time to tell you anything. You walked out.'

'Yes. Not only because of Matthew, but because I'd already decided to end it. It was getting too complicated. Too—emotional. But I missed you. I told myself I'd get over it. I wanted you, but I really rather despised myself. But when I saw that picture in the paper...'

Staring at her back, at the fall of thick, shiny hair, he apologised. 'I'm sorry, Githa... God, what a stupid thing to say. "Sorry"—what does that mean?' Straightening, as though it were an enormous effort, he continued doggedly, 'And when I saw Lucinda's smile of triumph, I felt sick.'

'Join the club. Go away, Henry. This is all pointless. You don't even like me.'

'Don't know you,' he corrected. 'I was a man at war with myself. I was attracted to you, wanted you, but I didn't want to like you, didn't want a commitment. And, in my more rational moments, couldn't believe I was behaving like a rampant schoolboy. I was thirty-six years old, rational, well educated, a man of sense—and I wanted you—' Breaking off, he gave a mirthless smile. 'Wanted you? That has to be the biggest understatement ever given; I was *desperate* for you. But Lucinda made sure she poisoned anything else. The kettle's boiling.'

Githa switched it off, turned back to face him.

'My mother is mortified at the way she treated you. She'd like to see you...'

'No.'

He sighed, examined her wan face. 'Why couldn't you have returned tomorrow when I would no longer have been jet lagged? Would have been able to think clearly?'

'Because I'm perverse.'

'Githa…'

'Sorry,' she apologised insincerely, 'but I don't want you here.'

'We had something good.'

'No,' she denied, 'we had something transient.'

'And you want something permanent?'

'No, I want something else.'

Hesitating a moment, he murmured quietly, 'You said you were in love with me…'

'*Were,*' she emphasised. 'Not any longer.' But she couldn't quite look him in the eyes as she said it. 'Go away, Henry.'

Turning her back, feeling old and used up, she relit the gas under the kettle, reached for the teapot with no clear idea of what she was doing. It was just something to pass the time, something to keep her occupied until he would go. Something to avert the possibility of blurting out that she might be pregnant.

'Githa…'

'Please go, Henry. Please, just go,' she repeated. She felt exhausted. Unable to cope any more.

Hearing his long sigh, she tensed, prayed he would leave quickly, and then he was gone, and she let her breath out on a long shudder. Slumping bonelessly, her eyes tight shut, she began to cry. She hadn't cried at all since it had started more than four months ago now. She'd come close once or twice, but now it was as though the dam had broken. All the fear, the worry, the pain. She felt betrayed and lost and lonely. But there was no one to see, and so it didn't matter.

Tired and aching, face all puffy, not thinking straight, not thinking clearly, she shoved dark glasses onto her nose and went out to get milk and bread—a mundane reality in a life that seemed to have wandered into nightmare.

She didn't want to see Henry again, she decided. He didn't love her, and even if he did he could hardly have a relationship with the girl who'd been victimised by his 'friend'. It would make life a little awkward, wouldn't it? She might, next time, do more than take photographs. And his mother was mortified because she'd been rude to a stranger.

And so the decision was made. She'd run away. Even if this hadn't happened, her relationship with him hadn't been going anywhere, had it? He didn't want to get married, have children—and she did. Probably was having a child. But her body ached for him. Her mouth felt cold without his kisses. And she didn't really think she was pregnant. Couldn't even begin to comprehend that she was, and so she shut it from her mind.

But she really did have to leave, didn't she?

Before she could become stupidly rational—hope— she went into the first estate agents she came to and put the house and contents up for sale. It would sell quickly, she was told. Houses in the mews always did.

Wandering slowly home, she dithered for a moment

or two outside the chemist's, and then determinedly went in and bought a pregnancy-testing kit. Best to be certain, wasn't it?

On her return, she asked Jenny to show prospective buyers around.

'But you *can't* leave,' she wailed miserably. 'I've only just got to know you! And I *like* living next door to you!'

'I like living next door to you too. But I have to go. A fresh start.' Knowing she was about to cry, she grimaced an apology and fled. No doubt Cindy would be pleased. She'd done all she'd set out to do.

The cheque from Varlane was with the post Jenny had been keeping for her, and so there was now no reason to wait. She'd start a new life. And by the time Henry came back she'd be somewhere else. Somewhere he couldn't find her. Always supposing that he wanted to.

The pregnancy-testing kit sat on the table, watching her, waiting, and with an irritated little gesture she snatched it up and took it up to the bathroom. It would show negative. Of course it would.

It didn't.

Disbelieving, she stared at the result. Reread the instructions. She *couldn't* be pregnant. Couldn't be. But there was only usually a mistake if it showed negative, not if it showed positive. And it definitely showed positive. Slumped on the edge of the bath, she stared before her with empty eyes. Now what did she do? She couldn't tell him. How could she tell him?

How long before he came back? If he came back. But there was no guarantee that he wouldn't, and so she must go tonight. Tossing the box into the bin, blanking her mind to everything, she walked out and into her bedroom, began hastily packing up her belongings—the designer dresses and suits that she would probably never need again, the expensive shoes and bags, and all the personal little things she'd accumulated over the years—the photograph album, things that had belonged to her parents. Had her mother been pleased when she'd discovered she was pregnant? But her mother had been married, loved...

Closing her eyes tight on a wave of anguish, she waited for the moment to pass and then began emptying out the drawer that contained over four months worth of victimisation. Tossing it all into a bin liner, she put it out for the dustman.

She couldn't be pregnant. She'd get another kit, test again.

Eyes still blank, disbelieving, she rang her agent to say she was moving, and to thank her for all she had done. Elaine didn't try to persuade her to stay on her books. Why should she? That photograph could surface again at any time. Newspapers often kept things in their files for future reference.

Well, that was one reference that was never going to have a future, because she had no intention of ever becoming famous again. Let the past go and move on—her aunt had always said that. And Githa missed her. It would have been nice to have sobbed it all out onto an ample breast, but the breast was long gone.

Conscious that Henry could arrive back at any time, she put everything by the front door, went to say goodbye to Jenny—and found Henry on her doorstep. He was still wearing his raincoat.

She tried to shut the door in his face, but he was quicker, easily held it against her frantic push.

'I didn't trust you not to run away,' he said quietly. 'Seems I was right,' he added as he eyed the mound of luggage. 'Cutting off your nose to spite your face, Githa?'

'It's my nose and my face, so I can do what I want with it. Go away.'

'No.'

'And I don't know why you're wearing that ridiculous raincoat! It isn't even raining!' She sounded hysterical because the fact of her pregnancy was there in her mind, her heart, on her tongue, just waiting to be said, blurted. And she mustn't. Couldn't.

'So it isn't,' he agreed.

Forcing her backwards, eyes intent, he stepped inside and closed the door. Githa hastily retreated.

'I don't want you here.'

'Don't you?'

'No. I thought you were going home to sleep.'

'I haven't been home. I've been walking, thinking, trying to clear my head. Why are you looking so terrified, Githa?'

'I'm not terrified!' Turning her back, she marched along to the kitchen.

'Agitated, then.'

'Neither am I agitated.'

'But you made up your mind to leave before I came back. Finish it. Why?'

Putting the kitchen table between them, she stared at him, refused to feel *anything*. '*You* finished it.'

'Yes. Something I bitterly regret. I once said I wouldn't beg—I lied. Can I make myself a coffee?'

'No.'

He ignored her, went to put the kettle on. 'You were intending to leave everything? Cups, plates?'

'I am leaving,' she corrected.

He sighed, looked momentarily helpless. 'I wanted what we had,' he continued quietly, 'and nothing more. And so I wouldn't allow myself liking, wouldn't allow—no, it's not a case of allowing, because the feelings were already there. It was a case of repressing them.'

'How very strong-minded,' she said admiringly.

'Yes. And you?' he turned to ask. 'Because you're repressing them too, aren't you?'

'Am I?'

'Yes. I missed you.'

'Did you?'

'Yes. Do you want a coffee? Tea?'

'No, thank you,' she declined politely, but she was shaking inside, frightened inside. Afraid of words, because one word could lead to another, could lead to her saying what she mustn't say. If she'd had time to get used to the idea before she saw him again... If it still hadn't been such a shock... Maybe—please, God—it wasn't true.

He made his coffee, carried it over to the table, put it down. 'Look at me, Githa.'

She turned away—and, for the first time since she had met him, didn't feel him behind her, and so gave an almighty start when he touched her shoulder.

Whirling away, she glared at him. 'Don't touch me!'

He frowned, examined her puffy face. 'What's happened?'

'Nothing!'

'Githa…'

'Nothing!' she shouted. 'Go away.' Hands gripped tightly on the work surface, she stared blindly at the Formica top. 'Go away,' she pleaded inaudibly.

'You're ill?'

'No,' she mumbled.

'Then, what?'

'Nothing.'

'Don't keep telling me ''nothing'',' he reproved, almost gently, 'when there's clearly something.' Grasping her shoulders, he turned her. 'Tell me.'

She frantically shook her head.

'Cindy came?' he guessed.

She shook her head again.

'Then, what? For God's sake, Githa, tell me, *what*?'

Shoving him away, eyes full of unwanted tears, she whispered brokenly, 'I think I'm pregnant.'

CHAPTER EIGHT

STUNNED into silence, Henry just stared at her. 'But you said…'

'I was on the pill, yes,' Githa agreed in a faint whisper. 'I was. I must have forgotten to take it or something—and don't *look* at me like that! I didn't do it on purpose! I don't expect—want—you to do anything about it!'

'No,' he agreed bleakly, 'because you weren't even going to tell me, were you? It is mine, I supp…? Of course it's mine,' he argued wearily. 'Sorry. I'm sorry. We'll get married…'

'Don't be absurd,' she interrupted shortly. 'People no longer get married because of a pregnancy. And it might be a mistake…'

'But you don't think it is?'

She shook her head, tears flooding her eyes once more, and from not wanting to talk at all she now didn't want to stop. She desperately needed to prevent any quixotic behaviour on his part. 'You don't want a wife, a family; you said so. Anyway, if I am, I could have a termination…'

'No!' he put in forcefully, and then looked slightly surprised at himself. 'No,' he repeated slowly. 'I don't want that.'

Neither did she. She didn't know why, and it certainly hadn't been her first reaction when she'd thought she was pregnant. She'd just thought she would—have it. 'I don't want you to marry me, Henry,' she repeated quietly. 'I think I'll have that tea now.'

'I'll make it,' he offered. 'Sit down, Githa.'

She obediently sat, clasped her hands on the table-top. It was a relief to have told him, she acknowledged. An unbelievable relief. It felt as though a great burden had been lifted. Finding a hanky, she blew her nose hard. Wiped away her tears.

Henry brought her tea over, placed it before her, then sat opposite.

'I didn't do it on purpose, Henry,' she said quietly.

'I know.' With a half-smile, he added, 'It's been a bit of a shock.'

'To me too.'

'You've seen a doctor?'

She shook her head.

'You must.'

'Yes.'

He sipped his cooling coffee, sighed. 'Why won't you marry me?'

'You know why.'

'Because you think I don't love you?'

'Because I know you don't.'

'A father,' he said softly. 'Oh, boy.'

'Yes. I'm sorry.'

'Don't be.' Watching her as she stared down into her tea, hands clasped round the cup, he felt an almost overwhelming feeling of protection. She looked so lost, so sad. And even with a puffy face and eyes she was still quite extraordinarily beautiful. 'My view of you was coloured by Lucinda's—intimations,' he said quietly, reflectively. 'So you see, I don't know the real you at all. The you before all this happened. And I would like to. Talk to me, Githa.'

'No, there isn't any point. I liked you, and you…'

'Betrayed you. As badly as Lucinda did,' he finished for her. 'I know that.'

With a twisted little smile, she began to trace imaginary patterns on the old wood of the table. 'She said it was disgusting.'

'What was?' he asked gently.

'Us. She saw us, you know. On the kitchen floor.'

'Did she?'

Snapping up her eyes, she demanded, 'Don't you *care*?'

'No, why should I? *I* didn't find it disgusting. Did you?'

With a helpless sigh, she resumed her tracings. 'I thought I was so lucky,' she continued with quiet bitterness. 'I *always* thought I was lucky.'

'Losing your parents when you were a baby can't be considered lucky.'

'No,' she agreed slowly, 'but I was lucky in that my aunt was prepared to look after me. She was kind, sweet, loving.' But this little baby wouldn't have an aunt, wouldn't even have proper parents—and that was so sad. She had always thought, hoped… Wiping away fresh tears, she hastily sipped her tea.

'It's all in the perspective, isn't it?' he continued.

'Lucinda considered herself *un*lucky that her parents died. Not lucky that she was taken in by a loving couple that she wouldn't allow to adore her.'

Surprised, she glanced up involuntarily. 'What?'

'I went to see them whilst you were away. They live in Norfolk now. Left the cottage for Lucinda to use. No one really knew them when they lived there. They were a quiet couple, kept themselves pretty much to themselves, and we only ever had Lucinda's version of what they were like. We were wrong about Lucinda, so perhaps we were wrong about them.'

'And were you?'

'Yes.'

'Did you tell them what had happened?'

'Some of it—not all. They didn't seem surprised. It seems whatever they gave her, whatever they said, did, was always wrong. She wanted the moon, and wouldn't settle for the stars. They weren't her parents, and she wouldn't accept them as such. They said she was always very bitter towards them, allowed everyone else to think they were unkind to her. They weren't. She never goes to see them. Never keeps in touch.'

'I know. I always felt so sorry for her.'

'So did everyone else.'

'And I thought we had a bond, because of our adoptions. An unbreakable one. But I was the lucky one. Loved. She used to come and stay with us—with my aunt and me—in the school holidays. My aunt spoiled her, tried to make up for her unhappy home life.'

'And her adoptive parents never tried to defend

themselves. Just grew quieter and eventually moved away. You look for the positive. Lucinda seemed to look for the negative. All hindsight, of course.'

'Yes. What will your mother say? About the baby? You will tell her?'

He gave an odd smile. 'Yes, I'll tell her. It would be very unwise not to. If she found out from other sources... My mother is very...I was going to say domineering, but that isn't quite true. She likes to be in charge. Thinks she knows what's best for everyone.

'It's a foolish man who mentions in front of my mother that he likes something, or someone, because if she agrees, likes the idea, she sets out to get it for them. On her terms. If she doesn't like the idea you never hear the last of it.

'I learned at a very early age not to tell my mother anything. I was forced into piano lessons for *years*, Githa, all because I happened to mention, casually, when I was five, that I liked to listen to the piano being played.'

She gave a faint smile. As he had intended. 'My father was forced into playing golf. It was good for him,' he added wryly. 'My father and I perfected the art of a straight face.'

'And so you got into the habit of never telling anyone anything. Pretended that you were cold and unemotional.'

'Yes. Self-preservation eventually became reality. I don't know when the change took place, I only know that it did. And that, until I met you, life had become very boring. No new, fresh exciting manuscripts to read. They all seemed mundane. No woman to excite my interest, much to my mother's disgust. Because she does, actually, yearn for a daughter-in-law. And when I tell her about the baby, as I must, be warned, Githa—she will descend on you. Try to take charge.'

'But she doesn't like me,' she argued. 'And so maybe she won't.'

He gave a rueful smile. 'Liking will have absolutely *nothing* to do with my mother's actions! Duty will. And she will like you,' he added gently. 'She will *blame* you for not standing up to her in the kitchen that day,' he added with another smile. 'She will blame me for not making things clear, for not seeing what Cindy was like. Will persuade herself that she always knew there was something odd about Lucinda. She will blame Tom for something or other—and she will overwhelm you with kindness. And probably arrange a wedding.'

Horrified, Githa looked up, stared at him. 'No.'

'Want to run away with me?' he asked softly. 'Where she won't find us?'

More tears filled her eyes, and she sniffed, shook her head. He reached across the table, gently touched her hand, and she hastily withdrew it.

'I feel as though my whole life has been a lie,' she whispered. 'I don't feel like a person any more.'

'And so you decided to leave. Begin again somewhere else.'

'Yes.' Her eyes were as empty as her smile.

'As what?'

'I don't know. Work on an airline desk somewhere,

a travel agent's.' But they were only words, there was
no enthusiasm in them. Just words to make life seem
normal again. 'I keep telling myself to pull myself
together. But it seems such an effort. And so I need
to be busy, *do* something, even if it's only running
away.'

'But fate hasn't been behaving at all well lately,
has it?' he asked with a small smile. 'I came back too
soon.'

'Yes. I don't want you here, Henry.'

'Because you can't forgive me?'

'No,' she denied honestly. 'Because I can't forgive
myself. I should never have had an affair with you. It
was stupid, irrational. You don't even like me.'

'Any more than you like me?' he returned softly.

'I don't *know* you. You would never *allow* me to
know you!' That hadn't stopped her falling in love
with him, though, had it?

'No, but I would like you to know me now.'

'Now is too late.'

'No, it isn't. Even apart from the baby, I need to
know you. Because of Lucinda, because of her ma-
nipulative skills, we did it the wrong way round. But
I wanted you. The very first time I saw you, despite
everything I thought I knew about you, I wanted you.
Like a child, like a fool. I cynically assured myself
that your appeal was your stock-in-trade, but it didn't
help. I wanted you. Just like that. I'd never felt like
that before. Didn't know I could. Raw sex,' he murmured wryly.

'Yes.'

'And you felt it too. Still feel it. Electricity jumps between us, encloses us in a magnetic field.'

'I *know* what it does, Henry!' she said irritatedly. 'I don't need it spelling out! But it isn't enough!'

'I know that. Now.' Reaching across the table, he again touched his fingers to the backs of her hands, and she immediately withdrew them, put them in her lap.

'Don't touch me, Henry.'

Linking his hands together on the table, as though it might stop the temptation, he gave a reluctant nod. 'But can we embark on a journey of getting to know each other? Of talking? Evenings out at the theatre? The ballet? Opera?'

'Opera?' she asked with horror. 'I can't think of anything more guaranteed to...'

'Depress you?' he asked with another smile. 'You don't like opera?'

'No.'

'And if I confess to a liking, I'm doomed?'

'Don't be silly. *Do* you?'

His amusement moved to his eyes. 'No,' he denied wryly. 'I don't much care for opera. Ballet?'

'No. And this won't work, Henry.'

'Why? Because I'm a constant reminder of Cindy's behaviour? If I hadn't seduced you, you would still have your job? Wouldn't be pregnant? Is that what you're saying?'

'No. You were just the peg to hang her grievances on. Oh, Henry, you're being obtuse! What I'm trying to ask, to say, is supposing—just supposing—we get to know each other, get to like each other, and supposing the relationship lasts longer than you envisaged or expected—what then?'

'You are considering one, then?' he asked softly. 'A relationship?'

'No,' she denied crossly, 'this is hypothetical. We're just *talking*.'

'I see. Then, *hypothetically*, I don't know. At the moment, I just want the *now* sorted out. There's a baby to consider...'

'I *know* there's a baby to consider!' Jumping to her feet, skidding her chair across the floor in her agitation, she continued, 'But I won't have a relationship with you just because there's a baby!'

'Our baby,' he corrected softly.

'All right, our baby! But I don't...'

'Need me?' he asked quietly.

'No! That isn't what I'm saying! But I could look after it myself. I'm quite capable...'

'Until it cries.'

'Stop it!' she shouted. 'Supposing Cindy finds out? Supposing she comes back?'

'She won't,' he said positively.

'But you don't *know* that!'

'Yes, I do. Sit down. Sit down, Githa; I'm sure getting yourself into a state isn't good for the baby.'

'You don't know anything about babies!' she said crossly, but nevertheless retrieved her chair and sat down.

'But I am going to learn.' He suddenly gave a funny smile—rather quirky, wry. 'I can't even believe

I'm having this conversation. Can't believe I'm accepting it as though...'

'You think I lied?' she demanded, incensed all over again.

He just looked at her until she subsided. 'No, Githa, I don't think you lied. Stop being so defensive. You didn't make it all by yourself—and I will *not* be shut out.'

'I wasn't trying to shut you out,' she mumbled. 'But you could hardly expect me to think you'd be pleased at the prospect. After all you said up at the cottage...'

'Can we please forget what I said at the cottage? I really don't think I can cope with having statements I made then hurled in my teeth every five minutes.'

'I'm not hurling them in your teeth. You *didn't* want children—you said so. Didn't want a wife! You said...'

'I know what I said. I have an excellent memory. Can we now get back to Cindy?'

She gave an irritated sniff.

'She won't be back,' he said firmly. 'She's gone to Australia.'

'Australia?'

'Yes. Asked the airline to transfer her. And if she does come back she knows that if she ever says anything to hurt you again, does anything, even *looks* as though she's going to do anything, she will regret it for the rest of her life. She *knows* that. She also knows that I don't make idle threats.'

Somewhat alarmed by the change in him, the grimness to his mouth, the hard light in his eyes, she whispered, 'What did you say to her?'

He shook his head. 'I shan't tell you.'

'Will you keep in touch with her?'

'No. But I need to keep in touch with you. Except there's to be no touching, is there?' he asked ruefully.

'No.'

'And you're insisting on that, are you?'

'Yes.'

'Because you can't think when I touch you? Any more than I can think when you touch me?'

'Henry—'

'Githa,' he interrupted gently. 'I don't intend to let you go without a fight.'

'I'm trying to be sensible.'

'I don't want you to be sensible.'

'You hurt me.'

'I know.'

'So I should go away, make a fresh start.'

'Should?'

She opened her mouth to speak, clarify it, but he forestalled her.

'But you keep thinking, Supposing there's a future in this? Supposing I'm throwing away something that could be special? I'm the baby's father...'

'Oh, Henry, *don't*!' she cried in distress. 'I didn't want it to be like this! Didn't want to be—affected by you. Didn't want to have a baby without marriage, without security, love. But...'

'Then give me a chance. Don't throw it away.

Don't let what happened stop you seeing me every day. Don't let her win.'

'I'm not letting her win. And who said I was going to see you every day?'

'I did. And how would you live if you went away?'

'The same as I've always lived! If you think for one moment that I expect or want you to support me, you're mistaken! I can get a job—for a while, at least—and when I have to give up working, well, I have some savings,' she said stiffly. 'And Etienne was generous in his severance cheque.'

'Don't live off your capital,' he warned. 'Find a job that pays enough to live on. Locally.' He gave a wide yawn, apologised. 'Sorry. Or move in with me,' he added casually.

Shocked, she just stared at him. 'No!'

He gave a small, mocking smile. 'No,' he agreed. 'A bit soon for that, is it? And what about the house? Still intending to sell it?'

'I don't know,' she replied crossly. Staring at him, eyes defiant, she demanded bluntly, 'What is it you *want*, Henry?'

Eyes holding hers, he said softly, 'You. It's all I can think about. Fantasise about.'

An alarming dip in her stomach, unable to tear her eyes away, she swallowed hard. 'I don't know if I can trust you,' she whispered.

'Trust me not to hurt you?'

'Yes.'

'I don't know that either,' he confessed. 'But don't you think it's worth a try?'

'I don't know.'

'Give me a month, Githa. Four weeks.'

'Without touching,' she insisted.

'Without touching,' he reluctantly agreed.

Staring at him, searching his eyes, his face—a face she desperately did want to touch—she sighed, said quietly, 'Go home and get some sleep.'

'And you won't run away?'

'No.'

'Promise?'

'Yes. But only for a month.'

He nodded, and got to his feet. Staring down at her, he gave another small smile. 'I'll ring you when I wake up.'

'Yes.'

Reaching out as though to touch her hair, he remembered his promise and ruefully withdrew the hand. 'This isn't going to be easy. Touching is an integral part of any relationship.'

'I know.'

'But you still insist on it?'

'Yes.'

'Fair enough. Don't forget to get in touch with the estate agent.'

'No.'

'And the doctor.'

'I won't.'

And then he was gone, and she didn't know if she was being a fool. A month without touching was going to be desperately hard. She could already feel tension building, but at the moment touching was *all* they had. And there had to be more. Had to be. But if there wasn't? Then she would go away. Have the baby on her own.

They managed a week. A fraught week. Githa had never really consciously realised how many times you touched other people in the course of a day—touched an arm to gain attention, touched to escort across a road, touched to remove a piece of fluff from a jacket. Shook hands, hugged, kissed. And there could be none of it. She'd said so.

By the following Friday she felt wrung out, on edge, nervous and jumpy like a young, unschooled horse. It felt as though there was a tight band round her chest, squeezing and squeezing her ribs, compressing her lungs—and Henry looked like a man on the edge of explosion. The first day it had been mildly amusing; by the seventh it wasn't.

They'd been to the theatre, to dinner, to lunch—never alone—and now, in a few minutes, he was picking her up to attend a literary dinner at the Sheraton where one of his authors was nominated for an award. And she felt sick with nerves and tension.

Staring at herself in the mirror, she thought a tumbril might be a better form of transport than a cab. Certainly she looked and felt as though she was going to her own execution. Her black dress had been wickedly expensive, courtesy of her Varlane days, but not one she would be able to wear for much longer.

Soon, her pregnancy would begin to show. The doctor's test had confirmed her own, and next month she would have a scan, and be able to see the baby. But at the moment it didn't feel real, and no bulge marred the exquisite lines of the long, figure-hugging black dress that exposed one lightly tanned shoulder and hung to her toes as though moulded only for her.

Black and gold shoes, black and gold clutch bag. Gold earrings, and a gold chain at her neck. She looked stunning. Her hair swung thickly—with movement, she thought with a wry little smile. Her face was made up with practised perfection. And she looked like a doll, she thought. Not like herself at all. Not *real*. If there were photographers there, if they recognised her… Supposing they'd seen the picture of her in the paper…?

The doorbell rang, and she jumped, fought to pull herself together. She couldn't spend her whole life being afraid she would be recognised. And anyway, coping with Henry was far more of an ordeal than any photographer might be.

Taking a deep breath, she walked slowly downstairs, opened the front door, and Henry just stared at her. His eyes were hungry. As were hers.

'Oh, God,' he whispered thickly.

She wanted to echo it, felt herself drawn as though by a magnet. Felt herself sway, and hastily gripped the door tight. She'd made the rules. She had to keep to them. Had to. She had never seen him in a dinner jacket, never seen him so formal, and she couldn't seem to drag her eyes away. He looked devastating, and, if you could ignore the expression in his eyes, the slight flush along his cheekbones, remote. Unattainable.

The cab driver hooted, and they both gave a small start.

'Shall we go?' he asked unsteadily.

'Yes,' she whispered.

The evening was a nightmare. She didn't remember what anyone said, wasn't even sure she heard. Didn't know which author won the award. Didn't even *notice* any photographers! She ate what was put before her, but her eyes remained fixed on Henry, only on Henry. Every nerve, every cell, was attuned only to him. When the interminable meal was over and they were free to mingle with the other guests, someone accidentally brushed against her. Without thought, she caught Henry's arm for balance, and he made a low sound like an animal in pain, drew in a sharp breath.

'Don't,' he murmured thickly. 'For God's sake, don't touch me. Not now, not here.' Finding her eyes with his, tension in every line of him, he fumbled his glass onto a nearby ledge, took hers. 'I'll get us a room.'

CHAPTER NINE

'NO,' GITHA whispered shakily, but without any conviction at all.

'Yes.' Turning from her, Henry summoned a waiter, had a quiet word, slipped him some money. The waiter nodded, hurried away. He took Githa's arm, and his hand was trembling, his breathing as constricted as hers. He led her out to the foyer, and across to the lift where the waiter was standing, holding a key in his hand. Henry took it, glanced at it, nodded, and almost pushed her into the lift.

'Henry...'

'Don't.' He stabbed a button, leaned back against the smooth sides, stared at the indicator, and she watched him, fear in her eyes. Fear and—need. Felt ill.

The lift halted and he straightened, didn't look at her, touch her, just stepped out, held the door open. Like an automaton, shaking, she followed him, walked along a silent, carpeted passage, watched with unseeing eyes as he opened a door—and she walked inside.

'Henry,' she whispered unsteadily, and he groaned, turned, hauled her into his arms.

'I made a promise,' he said against her hair, and

held her impossibly tight. 'But I can't keep it. This is destroying me.'

'I know,' she agreed raggedly, and he wrenched her head back, stared down into her lovely face—and began to kiss her with hunger and passion, with a week's worth of frustration.

And she was lost.

Clutching him as tightly as he was clutching her, she kissed him back with a feverish intensity that frightened her. She barely remembered them getting out of their clothes, only knew that suddenly she was naked, that he was naked, and was doing things to her that she had needed, wanted, for what seemed a very long time. They weren't coherent, rational, uttered just half-started sentences, with a desperate need to be close, closer.

His kisses were fierce, unrestrained, and she matched them, sought them. They were like animals, mindless beings that knew they needed this more than anything else in the world—this spiralling out of control that robbed them of thought.

He took her there, on the carpet, in front of the door. Took her to heaven. As she did him. Because she needed it as much as he did. And when he shuddered, dragged in a sobbing breath, she closed her eyes, held him tight, refused to let him go. As she had once before. That very first time.

She felt almost out of her own body, her own mind. Limbs shaking, lungs fighting for air, legs still wrapped round him, she held him tighter.

Face buried in her neck, her hair, voice muffled, he murmured, 'Githa...'

'Don't say you're sorry,' she begged unsteadily.

'No.'

'Don't say you couldn't help it, that I shouldn't have touched you. Don't say anything like that.'

'No.'

So they lay there for a few minutes longer, wrapped together impossibly tight. And probably looked extraordinarily stupid, she thought slightly hysterically.

'Henry?'

'Yes.'

'What *were* you going to say?'

'That I can't breathe.'

She giggled, a stupid hiccup of sound. 'Oh, Henry.'

'Mmm.'

Easing the pressure against his back, she allowed him to move, raise his head.

He stared down into her hazel eyes and his lips twitched. So did hers, and a rueful little smile lit her eyes.

'Not angry?'

She shook her head.

'I felt like a boiler with too much pressure building up.'

'And no safety valve,' she agreed softly.

'No.'

'I wanted you on my doorstep when you came to pick me up,' she confessed.

'I wanted you too. I've wanted you all week. I haven't done any work, haven't read any manuscripts.

Everything I touched felt like you. Everything I saw reminded me of you. I even went to the doctor, asked if it was all right to make love to a pregnant woman.'

'And what did he say?' she asked shakily.

'That it was all right. He seemed amused.'

'Yes. I don't think this is normal, do you?' she asked with a tiny little frown.

He grunted, gave a slow, absolutely devastating smile, and then he began to laugh. Resting his head against hers, he shook with laughter, tried to speak, and couldn't.

'It isn't funny, you know. We probably need counselling.'

He laughed even more—little whoops of merriment that made her smile, then grin, laugh with him, and when he managed some semblance of control he rolled onto his side, took her with him, gasped, 'How the mighty are fallen. I thought myself such a sensible fellow—and all I was was an arrogant fool,' he concluded softly. Eyes gentle—almost loving, she thought wistfully—he murmured, 'And whatever it is you have done to me, don't stop, will you?'

Eyes searching his, she shook her head, said a trifle sadly, 'I don't think I can.'

'But you want to?' he asked gently.

'No. What did you tell the waiter?'

'That you weren't feeling very well.'

'Did he believe you?'

'I doubt it. Let's go home. You haven't seen my apartment, have you?'

'No.'

'Come there with me now. Please?'

Home.

'What is it?' he asked gently.

She shook her head. 'I'll have a shower...'

'*We'll* have a shower.'

'Henry...'

'Shh. I can't let you go, Githa. I really don't think I can let you go. Please marry me.'

And she wanted to. Dear God, how she wanted to.

'Don't answer now.' Disentangling himself, he got to his feet, gently tugged her upright and led her into the bathroom. Finding a shower cap for her hair, he fitted it on, then grinned. 'Why do they make them so *large*?'

'I don't know,' she said helplessly.

'You look like a very sad bunny.'

'Do I?'

'Mmm. My very own sad bunny.'

Turning on the shower, he waited until the water ran warm, then tugged her to stand with him beneath the jets. He gently began to soap her—and it began all over again. That mindless, *hot* feeling, that helpless melting, everything blurring together, becoming unreal.

Gazing at him, she watched his eyes grow dark, slumberous, and groaned deep in her throat as she reached for him. 'This is so absurd,' she whispered against his wet chest. Unaware, uncaring that the water was soaking her face, destroying her make-up, wetting her hair beneath the ill-fitting shower cap, she impatiently wrenched it off, dropped it, and gave in to ecstasy—because soapy bodies slid together so beautifully.

'And now we have to start all over again,' he said throatily as he reached for the soap.

'Yes. Do you think we'll ever get out of the shower?'

'Yes, because I want you in my bed,' he said thickly. 'Want you in my life.' He handed her the soap. 'Best if you do it.'

'To me, or to you?'

'You,' he managed. Rinsing himself off, he stepped out, grabbed a towel, and wrapped it round his hips. Grabbing another, he towelled his hair, took a deep breath, and walked into the bedroom without looking back.

When she came out he was dressed, and her clothes were hung tidily over a chair. Voice still hoarse, smile rather wry, he said, 'I won't watch you dress. Can't watch you. So I will turn my back like a gentleman should, and get myself a much needed drink.' Bending to the mini bar, he took out a small bottle of Scotch and poured some into a glass.

'Do it quietly, Githa,' he reproved.

'Sorry?'

'I can hear the slither of your stockings, and it's...'

'Sorry,' she apologised hastily, and tried to be silent, but her hands were shaking so badly, her breathing laboured, and she remembered, once, not so long ago at the Hall, him saying that there was something so very arousing about being clothed when your partner was naked. There was also something very arousing about being naked whilst your partner was clothed, she discovered. And she wanted him. Again.

Suppressing it, fighting it, feeling weak and unsteady, she hurriedly pulled on her dress, smoothed it to fit, then walked across to use the hair-dryer that was mounted above the dressing table. She had no make-up left, no styling brush to style her hair, a man she couldn't leave alone, and a body that was still aching. She couldn't even be amused, laugh at herself—couldn't even speak, she thought. Drying her hair as best she could, she slipped on her shoes and found her bag.

'I'm ready,' she said quietly, and he turned to survey her.

Finishing his drink, he left the empty glass on the bar, and walked towards her. He didn't touch her, just stood in front of her, stared down into her wide eyes.

'Marry me,' he begged softly. 'Please marry me. I can't take another week like that. All those feelings I've suppressed over the years are swamping me. I love you, Githa. I don't want to spend the rest of my life without you— And don't cry,' he pleaded raggedly. 'Dear God, don't cry.'

Folding her in his arms, he held her against him, rested his cheek against her hair. 'All week I've wanted to put my hand on your stomach where a small life is growing. I want to be there for the scan, want to see my child. And I want his mother in my home, in my life, to keep safe, protect, love. I don't want to be alone any more, Githa.'

Face resting against his jacket, eyes closed, tears

soaking the expensive material—silent tears—she slid her arms round his waist. 'Oh, Henry.'

'Say yes,' he pleaded. 'I can't imagine a life without you now, but I can imagine laughter and loving, a baby to hold, to love. And I want more than anything for this child to know who I am. I didn't think I wanted any of that, was so arrogantly convinced of it, but I do, Githa. I want it more than anything on this earth. So say yes, please.'

People started out with less, didn't they? And made it work. She wanted it so badly. Easing herself away, she stared up into his face. Not arrogant any more, but soft, pleading, helpless. His grey eyes were steady, waiting, and it felt so good to be held protectively in the circle of his arms. He wasn't the sort of man to say he wanted something if he didn't. He could be arrogant, indifferent, tough, but if he *did* love her...

'Yes,' she whispered.

He closed his eyes, took a tiny little breath, pulled her back against him, and buried his face in her hair. 'Because?' he prompted.

'Because I love you,' she said simply.

Raising his head, he stared down into her lovely face once more. 'Smile for me, Githa,' he demanded unsteadily.

She tried, but it didn't come off very well. 'I feel a bit...'

'So do I. And I don't want to move, leave, in case the mood is broken, in case you start having second thoughts.'

'I've finished with second thoughts.'

'Have you?'

'Yes. From now on I'm only going to have first ones,' she promised him.

'Good. Shall we stay the night?'

'Sleep here?'

'Oh, no,' he denied softly, throatily. 'I don't intend for us to sleep.'

Eyes trapped by his, she finally found a smile.

MILLS & BOON®

Next Month's Romances

♡

Each month you can choose from a wide variety of romance novels from Mills & Boon. Below are the new titles to look out for next month from the Presents™ and Enchanted™ series.

Presents™

THE DIAMOND BRIDE	Carole Mortimer
THE SHEIKH'S SEDUCTION	Emma Darcy
THE SEDUCTION PROJECT	Miranda Lee
THE UNMARRIED HUSBAND	Cathy Williams
THE TEMPTATION GAME	Kate Walker
THE GROOM'S DAUGHTER	Natalie Fox
HIS PERFECT WIFE	Susanne McCarthy
A FORBIDDEN MARRIAGE	Margaret Mayo

Enchanted™

BABY IN A MILLION	Rebecca Winters
MAKE BELIEVE ENGAGEMENT	Day Leclaire
THE WEDDING PROMISE	Grace Green
A MARRIAGE WORTH KEEPING	Kate Denton
TRIAL ENGAGEMENT	Barbara McMahon
ALMOST A FATHER	Pamela Bauer & Judy Kaye
MARRIED BY MISTAKE!	Renee Roszel
THE TENDERFOOT	Patricia Knoll

H1 9802

Available from WH Smith, John Menzies, Martins, Tesco and Asda

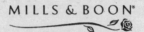

PARTY TIME!

How would you like to win a year's supply of Mills & Boon® Books? Well, you can and they're FREE! Simply complete the competition below and send it to us by 31st August 1998. The first five correct entries picked after the closing date will each win a year's subscription to the Mills & Boon series of their choice. What could be easier?

BALLOONS	BUFFET	ENTERTAIN
STREAMER	DANCING	INVITE
DRINKS	CELEBRATE	FANCY DRESS
MUSIC	PARTIES	HANGOVER

S	O	E	T	A	R	B	E	L	E	C
T	E	F	M	U	S	I	C	D	D	H
S	U	I	V	Z	T	E	Y	R	A	A
N	E	N	T	E	R	T	A	I	N	N
O	B	V	E	R	E	H	K	N	C	G
O	J	I	F	O	A	L	R	K	I	O
L	M	T	F	V	M	P	U	S	N	V
L	P	E	U	Q	E	N	Z	S	G	E
A	W	G	B	X	R	C	T	B	Y	R
B	F	A	N	C	Y	D	R	E	S	S

C8B

Please turn over for details of how to enter...

HOW TO ENTER

Can you find our twelve party words? They're all hidden somewhere in the grid. They can be read backwards, forwards, up, down or diagonally. As you find each word in the grid put a line through it. When you have completed your wordsearch, don't forget to fill in the coupon below, pop this page into an envelope and post it today—you don't even need a stamp!

Mills & Boon Party Time! Competition
FREEPOST CN81, Croydon, Surrey, CR9 3WZ
EIRE readers send competition to PO Box 4546, Dublin 24.

Please tick the series you would like to receive if you are one of the lucky winners

Presents™ ❑ Enchanted™ ❑ Medical Romance™ ❑
Historical Romance™ ❑ Temptation® ❑

Are you a Reader Service™ Subscriber?   Yes ❑   No ❑

Mrs/Ms/Miss/Mr ....Intials ....
(BLOCK CAPITALS PLEASE)

Surname...

Address ....

....

....Postcode.....................

(I am over 18 years of age)   C8B

HEATHER GRAHAM POZZESSERE

If Looks could Kill

Madison wasn't there when her mother was murdered, but she *saw* it happen. Years later, a killer is stalking women in Miami and Madison's nightmare visions have returned. Can FBI agent Kyle Montgomery catch the serial killer before Madison becomes his next victim?

"...an incredible storyteller!"—LA Daily News

1-55166-285-X
AVAILABLE FROM FEBRUARY 1998

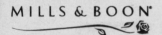

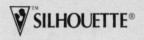